To Robert

Best wishes for

a Happy Birthday

Auntie Lizzie, Uncle Dave
& Helen.

Tomay is Loyal

by the same author

THE RING OF FORTUNE
THE THREE QUEENS

TOMAY IS LOYAL

by

Margaret Priestley

illustrated by

Philip Hepworth

FABER & FABER LIMITED
24 Russell Square
London

First published in mcmli
by Faber and Faber Limited
24 Russell Square London W.C.1
Printed in Great Britain by
Purnell and Sons Limited
Paulton (Somerset) and London

Contents

Contents

Aunt Marion brings News

IT WAS a wild night.

Katharine Holt drew back the curtains and opened the window, and at once a gust of wind hurled the rain in her face and flung the curtains into an abandoned dance.

"Shut the window at once, Katharine!" ordered Mistress Heebes sharply. "What do you think you are doing? Sometimes you are quite unaccountable!"

"I'm cold!" whined Fanny, with an exaggerated shiver.

Kate slammed the window shut. It had been briefly refreshing, the beat of the storm outside, for the room was hot and stuffy. She said meditatively:

"I think our lives are like that. We shut ourselves up in boxes, and all kinds of things go on outside that we know nothing about."

Fanny giggled.

"What things you do say, Kate!" she exclaimed.

"Get on with your work, Katharine," ordered

Mistress Heebes. "And you, Fanny, my dear, draw near to the fire. I fear you may have caught a chill as a result of your cousin's thoughtlessness."

Kate did not raise her head at this reproach. She picked up her sampler with a sigh, and spread it on her knee. Usually she enjoyed doing needlework, but tonight she had no enthusiasm for it. The little picture she had designed herself looked prim and petty.

There was a rustle of skirts outside the door, and it opened to admit her aunt. She and Fanny and Mistress Heebes rose and curtseyed respectfully, then Fanny cried out:

"Mama! Why are you wearing black? Has somebody died?"

Aunt Marion dabbed at her eyes with a wisp of lace handkerchief, and, sitting down in the big chair, drew her daughter close to her.

"Children," she said dramatically, "a terrible thing has happened. Something that will prostrate the whole country with grief."

"The King?" gasped Kate.

"No, Kate. Please do not interrupt," Aunt Marion said irritably; and she turned to Fanny. "My darling, I know you will be very distressed," she said, "for you are so sensitive; but you must try to be brave." She paused for effect, dabbing her eyes again before she went on.

"The Queen and the dear little baby, our prince, are both dead of a fever."

"Oh, ma'am, how terrible!" Mistress Heebes threw up her hands, suitably impressed. "What a dreadful tragedy!"

"Shall I have to wear black?" whined Fanny. "I hate black!" and she began to cry.

"Poor darling, so sensitive!" Aunt Marion stroked Fanny's golden curls. Then she continued, speaking to the governess, who seemed to be the most satisfactory listener: "They say His Majesty is quite out of his mind, he is so ill with grief, and the Duke of Craglands has been appointed Protector of the Kingdom until he is well again."

"Well, ma'am, I'm sure that is a good thing," said Mistress Heebes.

"A very good thing indeed, Mistress Heebes," Aunt Marion condescended to agree. "Rupert Mountmaris of Craglands is a strong man, and a firm ruler, and, as Mr. Holt always says, what the country wants now is a strong hand. But we women cannot understand politics, can we? Katharine! You are not getting on with your needlework."

"I beg your pardon, Aunt," Kate hurriedly went on stitching, as she added, "Joe says that Mountmaris is only out for himself."

Aunt Marion stared.

"Joe?" she queried in astonishment. "And who, may I ask, is Joe?"

"Please, Aunt, the stable boy," said Kate. "He comes from the north, and he is a friendly, sensible boy. David and I often talk to him."

"The stable boy!" exclaimed Aunt Marion. "You ungrateful little miss! Here are your uncle and I making great sacrifices to bring two penniless orphans up with our own daughter, and to give them a good education, and they have the impertinence to spend their time consorting with the stable boy!"

Kate suddenly felt defiant. She dropped her needle-work on the floor and stood up, facing her aunt with her hands behind her back.

"David and I think," she said firmly, "that Joe teaches us better things than Mr. Lane or Mistress Heebes."

"Go to your room!" exclaimed Aunt Marion. "And no supper! Do you hear? Such ingratitude! It's too much!" She began to sob loudly, making great play with her handkerchief, while Mistress Heebes and Fanny hastened to minister to her.

Kate left the room quietly. She might have banged the door and rushed upstairs in a fury, as she had done many times before, but tonight she had no heart for it. She knew that her rash words would cost Joe his job, and would involve David, her brother, in trouble as well as herself. Oh, it was hopeless! hopeless! Kate could see nothing ahead but long dreary years of subjection to Mistress Heebes, Aunt Marion and Fanny, with Uncle Clarence booming authoritatively at her from time to time when she had been particularly rebellious. The prospect was leaden-grey, too heavy, too blank for tears and it was in vain to storm about it, for she had long ago learned that storming was no use. It was just inevitable, her life, planned by some inexorable and unjust fate.

If only Mother and Father hadn't been killed during the Uralian occupation! Had they thought, Kate wondered, when they had given their lives so bravely for the country they believed in, of the misery of their orphaned children? "No, that isn't fair," she thought sturdily, as she trailed up the last flight of stairs. "They were right, and I'm proud of them."

Then there was their mother's brother, their Uncle Hugh. If only they had been able to go and live with him! He might be an eccentric scholar, poverty-stricken and foolish, as Uncle Clarence said, but he surely could not be worse than Uncle Clarence himself with his pompousness and his tyranny.

Kate opened the door of her little attic bedroom and went inside. It was cold, and she could hear the rain beating on the roof. She remembered suddenly, with self-reproach, that the queen was dead, and the little crown prince whose birth had caused general rejoicing nearly a year ago. Her small troubles became very insignificant beside those of the king.

It was not that King Roderick was a popular or romantic figure. Young, lonely, and suspicious of everyone, he had always appeared pathetic rather than glamorous. There had been a brief time soon after his marriage to the gracious and charming sister of the Insulan King, when he had been cheered wherever he went, but that was not long after the Uralians had been driven from the country and the people had been all agog to idolize somebody. It could have been either the Prince of Tomay, who had virtually freed them, or the young King; but Tomay, disgusted with court life, had soon retired to his own province, and the King had somehow failed them, and so although they had always acclaimed the Queen, the people had had to turn elsewhere to find their hero.

They had found Lord Rupert Mountmaris, the only son of the great Duke Steven of Craglands. Handsome, gifted, a born leader, Lord Rupert had carried all before him, and now he had succeeded to his father and become the most powerful man in the kingdom. It had even been whispered that the King was king only in name—and now the Queen was dead, and her son, and Mountmaris was Protector.

Kate had never been particularly interested in the doings of the great, but she had often had to listen to her uncle holding forth on the virtues of this man, or the vices of that one, and now she had heard through Joe the stable boy whisperings of a different point of view. Uncle Clarence was a fervent admirer of the new Protector, but Joe hinted that he was an unscrupulous and ambitious man, tyrannical to his tenants in the north, and cruel when his will was opposed.

Kate's thoughts were interrupted by the abrupt knock that always heralded her brother David. He burst into the room, his dark face intense and earnest.

"Kate, have you heard?"

"Yes," she nodded. "And I've done a stupid thing!"

"I know," he laughed. "Aunt was fluttering about it downstairs. Never mind, Joe has gone anyway! He left for Craglands tonight. He told me he was finished with the city."

"I don't blame him," Kate said fiercely. "I wish we could go."

"Kate, do you know what this means?" David said. "It means Mountmaris is virtually King! The White Guard that he initiated as a chivalrous band of knights to protect the King are nothing but a private gang of bandits!"

"I expect," said Kate, "the King will soon be better."

"He won't get the chance," cried David excitedly, tossing a lock of hair out of his eyes. "And do you know,

14

Kate, that after Tomay, Mountmaris is the next heir? His mother, the dowager Duchess of Craglands was Princess Anne, a daughter of the old King Henry. He is another grandson—and *he* won't stop at anything."

Kate, always absorbed by personal matters rather than by great issues of state, found it hard to visualize the danger that David saw. What did it matter, after all, who ruled the country? Mountmaris was probably most efficient. Anyway, the White Guard always made a fine show when troops of them rode through the streets. She thought David was exaggerating, but she did not say so, because she knew he would be hurt. Instead she changed the subject by offering him half a piece of ginger-bread she had hidden under her pillow.

David the young idealist turned back into a boy again as he chewed the ginger-bread, and the two of them sat side by side on the bed and mimicked Fanny and their pompous uncle. It made them laugh till Kate nearly swallowed a crumb the wrong way, and David had to thump her on the back.

They were rather alike to look at, both being skinny and long-legged, with thick dark-brown hair which fell into elf-locks, pale pointed faces and dark-grey eyes that could be stormy. David was a dreamer, full of ideas and theories; Kate strictly practical and influenced entirely by personal relationships. He was more even-tempered than she, perhaps because ideas are less irritating than people. Uncle Clarence called Kate a termagant.

"Fanny will be coming up here soon to see what we are up to," said Kate, when the last crumb of ginger-bread had gone and she had recovered her sobriety.

David nodded. "We'd better go to bed," he said.

"We don't want another row straight away. It gets so monotonous."

He went, philosophically, and Kate undressed, feeling far more cheerful.

"If I lived among people I liked," she thought ruefully, "I might be quite passably good-tempered!"

II

A Cry out of the Dark

KATE woke quite suddenly in the middle of the
night, with the feeling that she had heard somebody calling. She sat bolt upright in bed and
listened so hard that every part of her was still and tense,
but she could hear nothing but the spasmodic howling
of the wind and the swift lashing of the rain.

"It must have been a dream," she told herself sensibly,
and to her annoyance found that she was trembling. "It
is cold," she excused herself as she cuddled down into
bed again.

She settled herself in her most comfortable position,
and closed her eyes tight, but she could not sleep, for
through the sound of the storm she kept hearing things.
She thought she heard the crack of a musket shot, a
shout, and then, later, the clatter of horses' hoofs. It
made her sit up again, tensely alert, for a moment. Then
there was a lull in the storm, and she heard nothing—
nothing at all.

"A lot of nonsense!" she exclaimed aloud, because the
silence was in a way more terrifying than the noises she

had imagined. The sound of her own rather quavery voice was not very reassuring, and she wished her aunt would allow her to have a candle in her room. A little light would have been very comforting. The rain was beating fiercely again, like myriads of little people clamouring angrily to get in. Kate imagined them as queer little bedraggled grey elves with dripping fingers.

"Stay out!" she told them; and as if in answer to her defiance the rain ceased suddenly, and in the ensuing stillness she heard again the sound that must have awakened her—a long, heartbroken wail, faint and distant.

For one moment Kate stayed as if frozen, then, like lightning, she was out of bed and had scampered across to the door and through it into the corridor. Moving like a scared ghost on her bare feet, for even in her terror she instinctively took the precautions necessary not to awaken the family, she fled to David's room and flung herself upon his bed.

"David! David!" she whispered through chattering teeth. "Wake up! Oh, please wake up! I heard a banshee!"

"Good heavens, Kate!" he exclaimed sleepily and rather crossly. "You landed right on my legs. Banshee? There aren't such things."

"But I heard one, I tell you!" persisted Kate. "It woke me, and then I heard it again. I know I did."

"It must have been the storm," said David. "The wind does make queer noises."

"There it is again!" Kate clung to his arm as she spoke. She felt him stiffen as he heard the thing. Then he relaxed and said sturdily:

18

"Cats, that's what it is! Let's open the window and listen again."

"Cats, of course! Why didn't I think of it before?" Kate began to giggle a little with relief. They opened the window and leaned out, David balancing a glass of water to throw at the offenders. The sound came right from the courtyard below, an angry and despairing cry. David raised the glass, but Kate caught his arm.

"It's a baby," she said.

"Oh, nonsense," said David; but even as he said it he knew that she was right. Down there in their uncle's courtyard there was a baby.

"Poor little thing," said Kate, becoming practical at once. "We'd better go down and get it."

"Look here, do be quiet, Kate," protested David, as he shut the window. "Fanny's just along the passage, and you know what a light sleeper she is."

"I'll be like a mouse," Kate whispered. "Lend me your other cloak. Come on!"

They crept out into the passage and down the back stairs. This was an adventure too interesting to be more than pleasantly frightening. Outside the cook's door they listened for a moment and heard her snoring steadily. Down on the ground floor they felt fairly safe, and they groped their way to the kitchen and went in. The fire was still smouldering in the grate. David found some dry sticks in the wood-box and flung them on the embers; by the light of the flames the kitchen looked mysteriously enormous. They went to the back door and cautiously drew back the heavy bolts. The door swung inwards slowly, creaking enough, Kate thought, to awaken the whole household, and the room was suddenly filled with the wind. The child's cry, piercing and urgent, seemed to come from only a few feet away.

Kate, all her fear gone because of an overwhelming sense of pity, darted out into the blackness. Almost at once she tripped over something and fell on her face. As she got to her feet shakily she heard a long sigh.

"Oh, I'm sorry," she said, "I'm sorry I fell over you."

There was no answer for a moment, then someone whispered very faintly: "The Prince . . . ."

"David," said Kate; and in a moment her brother was beside her. He had paused in the kitchen to light a lanthorn, and by its flickering light they saw a man lying on his back in the mud, his eyes staring strangely out of his white face. Kate lifted his head gently.

"Oh, David," she gasped, "he's terribly hurt. We must get him inside and fetch a doctor."

"No, no," the man spoke again, faintly, "you mustn't do that! Don't call anybody. But the Prince—you must take him."

"The Prince?" queried Kate. "I don't understand—the Prince is dead."

"No, he is here," said the man. "I took him away from that traitor—before they could kill him."

Kate slipped her cloak under his head, and said firmly: "You mustn't give up. We'll look after you and the baby. Wait!"

She fled into the house and found a decanter of wine and a cup and a clean towel. She ran back with them, afraid that his life would have slipped away while she was gone, but his eyes were still open and watching. David had found the child and quieted it. He wrapped it in his cloak while Kate poured some of the wine into a cup.

They held the man's head and he drank slowly. Then Kate bound his wounded thigh with strips of the towel.

"I don't believe it's serious," she said, wondering at her own efficiency. "You've lost a lot of blood, that's why you're so weak."

"You are a gem of a nurse," replied he, speaking more strongly now.

"We must get you inside," said David. "We'll try not to hurt you."

"I think," said the stranger, "that if I had an arm round each of your shoulders and got on my good leg, I might make it."

They took the baby in first and made him comfortable on the settle. He was quiet now, exhausted by his crying. Then they got the wounded man in somehow and laid him down on the floor with a cushion under his head. He closed his eyes and Kate was afraid he had fainted again.

"What do we do now?" she asked David. "Who is he, d'you think? Is it really true, what he says?"

David fetched the wine from outside, and the lanthorn, which he set upon the table. They revived the wounded man with some difficulty, and when he was looking at them intelligently again, David asked: "Please, will you tell us who you are?"

"My name is John Forester," he answered. "Tell Joe I'm here, will you? Joe Angus."

"Joe has gone," said David. "He left for Craglands this evening. Couldn't we do something?"

Forester groaned.

"It was Joe I needed," he said. "He would have taken the prince to Tomay—Tomay—that's the only safe place for him. Tomay is loyal. But what can you do? You are just children—and, for all I know, supporters of that traitor Mountmaris."

"No, we're not!" David broke in eagerly. "We're friends of Joe's, and we'll help you. Won't we, Kate?"

"I don't know anything about Mountmaris," said Kate, who was nursing the baby, and had started taking off his wet clothes, "or about who is a traitor and who isn't, but I'm not going to let anyone hurt this baby. Look—he's smiling, after all he's been through. I'll take him anywhere where he'll be safe."

The baby was sitting up on her lap like a small naked god, and meditatively sucking his finger. The firelight made his skin warm gold. There was a gleam of hope in Forester's eye as he raised himself on his elbow and looked at Kate.

"Good girl!" he said. "And do you think your parents will help? You'd better wake them, for there'll be a house-to-house search before morning. I shall be found, and it will be prison for me, I fear."

"We have no parents living," said David slowly. "Our aunt and uncle wouldn't help. They believe in Mountmaris. No, Kate and I must do this by ourselves. We have an uncle in Tomay. We can go to him."

Forester looked worried again.

"It's a crazy idea," he said. "Two children! But I think we'd better try it. Only you must be quick."

"Would you mind telling us," asked Kate gently, "why you had to bring the little Prince away? Then we should know where we were a little—you see . . ."

"Yes," Forester said bitterly, "it must be difficult for you to believe my story. I was the Queen's equerry. When she died, my wife, who was the little Prince's nurse, was ordered by Mountmaris's secretary, Captain Varek, to take the child to our apartment and keep him secretly, and she obeyed, because she is afraid of Varek. Everyone is. When we heard that the child's death had been announced publicly and to the King, we knew something was wrong, and I got an audience with the King, who was overjoyed to find his son was still alive but seemed to be himself quite helpless in the duke's hands. He instructed me to take the child at once to Tomay, and gave me a letter. So when Varek came to demand the Prince I left with him by the window while my wife talked to Varek at the door. But some of Mountmaris's white wolves saw me going, and gave chase."

"Did they know you came here?" asked David.

"I don't think they followed me here—no—I came because I thought Joe could help me. But it's life and death. You must go at once."

It was crazy—but there was the Prince sleeping now, in Kate's lap, and they must go.

Upstairs the family still slept. Kate was seized with an insane desire to laugh. She spread the baby's tiny garments before the fire, and David threw on more wood.

"I'll get our things," he said quietly then, and slipped away.

Forester went on speaking, slowly, as if he was very tired.

"His name is Louis," he said, "and in my wallet there is a letter to the Prince of Tomay. There are some people by the North Gate who will help you on your way. Their name is Ladbrooke. Tell them you come from me."

Kate nodded. She left the child sleeping on the settle, wrapped in a cloak, and took the letter from his wallet.

Then Forester seemed to drowse. David brought down a bundle of clothes and he and Kate dressed hastily before the fire. They bundled the baby in shawls, and Kate picked him up.

They stood ready to depart, and looked down at John Forester; there he lay on the floor, sleeping now, and breathing quietly.

"Don't wake him," whispered Kate. "Oh, I do hope he'll be all right."

Then the two children and the stolen Prince slipped out into the dark.

III

A Strange Friend and a Strange Lodging

It was only when they were hurrying up the street that Kate realised what madness the whole thing was. She faltered for a moment.

"David," she said, "are we mad?"

"Mad? Quite mad," he said. "But we can't go back."

Kate wondered wildly if she could be dreaming, but no—there was the baby, warm and heavy in her arms. The familiar houses of the respectable street seemed to have disclaimed them already. They were tramps, outcasts, and the shuttered windows were like Aunt Marion's eyes when she closed them in horror.

"We are strangers already," thought Kate. Aloud she said: "Do you know the way to the North Gate?"

"Revelry Row goes up to it," said David, "but I think we'll stay in the lesser streets. We can't afford to meet anyone. Two children out at this hour would be sure to arouse comment. We simply mustn't let the White Guard get suspicious of us."

They cut down an alley. The wind dropped somewhat,

and the rain lessened, so that a shred of a sickle moon shone out briefly between the clouds, showing them their way over the wet cobblestones.

David said: "What do babies eat?"

"Oh, milk and things. He must be about eleven months, so he'll eat food too. He has some teeth."

"Humph!" exclaimed David. "It's lucky you know. I hope we don't poison it by mistake. The things have delicate stomachs, don't they?"

"We'll manage," said Kate.

"Shall I carry him for a bit?" suggested her brother, and Kate was glad to rest her aching arms. David took the child gingerly, and they went on.

"Forester gave me a letter for the Prince of Tomay," said Kate.

David let out an exclamation. "You'll have to go a long way to deliver that. He's in Mir."

"The Prince of Tomay? How do you know?"

"Joe told me. He was an admirer of his. He said that the Mirans had once made the Prince promise that if ever they were in trouble he would give them his advice and help, and so when they had some insurrection or other he had to go over." But he added doubtfully: "I don't know, Kate. What if the Prince of Tomay were as unscrupulous as Mountmaris? Uncle Clarence seems to think he is a wicked person, and Prince Louis being out of the way would benefit him too. He is the next in the line of succession—closer to the throne than Lord Rupert, even."

Kate nodded. "But Forester said: 'Tomay is loyal'," she pointed out.

"He may have meant the province, not the man," suggested David, "or he may even have been tricking us."

26

"But I must deliver the letter," said Kate, "even if we don't hand over the baby. And I don't believe John Forester was dishonest, because he seemed a very nice sort of person."

"By what judgment?" David laughed at her. "Feminine intuition, I suppose. Oh, come, Kate, you only isaw him for a few minutes. A nice sort of person ndeed! How could you possibly know?"

"You may scoff, but I'll bet you find I'm right," said Kate. "However, perhaps the best plan would be to find Uncle Hugh and see if he will help us."

"Yes," agreed David; and added rather grimly, "but he is an unknown quantity too. It all comes down to this, Kate, that we can trust nobody but ourselves."

They walked on in silence for a long while, and mercifully met no one except a night watchman, and they hid in a doorway while he went by. Once they heard the clatter of hoofs and saw a detachment of the White Guard ride across the mouth of the alley they were in.

Kate shivered, and made David give her back the baby, because she found his warm weight comforting. They were very much alone, the three of them, in the sleeping city. Kate thought how terrifying it must be to be a criminal, a fugitive, with every man's hand against yours. The White Guard had always seemed to her dashing and romantic, but now they were menacing. White wolves, John Forester had called them, and they had shot at him and wounded him.

"We're near the river now," said David softly, "and the North Gate is on the other side of the old north bridge; but we must find somewhere to hide till dawn. We can't enquire for these people called Ladbrooke at this hour. Perhaps among these warehouses we could find a hiding-place."

Then, quite suddenly, a man with a lanthorn came round the corner and faced them.

"Now then, now then!" He raised the lanthorn and shone it on their faces. "What are you doing here?"

Then he started. He had expected urchins, but he saw two well-dressed children with pale, weary faces.

"Now, now, young master and mistress," he went on more kindly, "what are you doing here? You should be in your beds. Where do you live?"

Kate was speechless. David opened his mouth to make some kind of answer, but he was saved the trouble, for there was a shrill, derisive whistle, and something flew through the air and accurately removed the watchman's hat. With an exclamation of fury he turned, and, cursing fluently, gave chase to his invisible assailant. David grabbed Kate's arm and dragged her hastily in the opposite direction. In a few minutes they were both crouching behind a pile of timber on one of the wharves.

They heard the watchman grumbling as he returned, and saw him flashing his lanthorn about, evidently looking for them. Then he appeared to give it up, and went away along the empty wharf.

"My goodness, that was lucky!" gasped Kate. "Well, I've always wanted an adventure, and now that I've got it I'm not sure that I like it!"

David was silent. He realised more clearly than his sister, who always lived in the present, what a tremendously difficult task they had undertaken.

"Not like it?" chuckled a hoarse little voice from just above them. "I'll say yer don't!"

Both children looked up, startled, and saw a small, monkey-like figure perched on a pile of timber, silhouetted against the sky.

"Who are you?" gasped Kate, holding the baby close.

"I'm Tommy, that's who I am." He scrambled down beside them. "Run away?" he asked laconically.

"Yes," answered David. "Was it you knocked the watchman's hat off? If so we must thank you."

"My, don't we talk grand!" Tommy imitated David's voice mincingly, then he went on: "That wasn't nothing. I see you were green."

"Do you live around here, Tommy?" asked Kate eagerly. "D'you know some people called Ladbrooke?"

"I lives round here," the boy admitted, "but I ain't in social life, as it were. Don't know your Ladbrookes, but

29

I could find out—I lives with the gang—under the bridge. Like to see?"

"No, thank you," said David hastily, "we can't. You see, they wouldn't all be like you. Someone might give us away. We've got to go secretly, or they'll fetch us back. But show us somewhere where we can hide safely till morning, and I'll give you a silver piece, which is all the money I've got."

Tommy seemed to be considering, then he motioned to the others to follow, and he set off down the wharf.

"Can we trust him?" Kate whispered.

"We'll risk it," answered David in the same tone. "I think he's trustworthy."

They were led down a steep flight of steps and into a sort of basement under a great warehouse. It was very dark, and smelled fusty.

"Wait," said their guide in a hoarse whisper; and they stood still.

"I'm a bit scared," confessed Kate. David squeezed her arm comfortingly.

They heard Tommy scuffling about, then a light flickered, and he came towards them carrying a lighted candle-end.

" 'Ere's yer palace," he said, and holding the light high he proudly showed them a great vaulted cellar, empty and dusty, with incredible cobwebs slung between its stone pillars.

"Th–thank you, Tommy," said Kate doubtfully, and her voice echoed queerly in that great empty place.

"It's a wonderful refuge!" exclaimed David with forced heartiness, handing over the silver piece. Tommy bit this to see if it was good, grinned, and put it in his pocket.

"I'll be along in the morning with news of your Ladbrookes," he said, and he looked curiously at the baby. "Who's he?" he asked.

"Baby brother," said David hastily. "We couldn't leave him behind."

"Could you possibly bring some milk for him, Tommy?" asked Kate anxiously. "If you can, I'll give you my gold bracelet."

"I'll see if I can," said Tommy with a wink.

"Good night, then."

"G'bye." He vanished into the gloom, having left the candle-end on the floor by them.

"Well," exclaimed David, "what a place! But I suppose we ought to be grateful for it."

"I think it's terrifying," sighed Kate. "And that candle-end won't last long, either. After that goes out I'm going to feel very creepy indeed."

"Well, it isn't for long." David tried to comfort her. "We'll sit here on these boxes and try to doze."

Kate shuddered involuntarily and held the baby close. He was still sleeping peacefully, but she thought his small face looked rather pinched in the flickering light.

David found a corner among a pile of broken crates, and arranged them so that he and Kate could sit with their backs supported. They crouched close together, for it was very cold.

Shivering, Kate watched the sputtering candle until it guttered and went out. Then she stared into the darkness with aching eyes.

Once or twice she heard the noise of rats scampering across the floor, and shrank closer to her brother. She would have given anything to have been back in her

31

little room, and to have heard the reassuring sounds of Aunt Marion's plaintive voice, Uncle Clarence's pompous booming, or Mistress Heebes's nagging.

"Oh, why did we ever come?" she wondered. "We're mad! We can't go to Tomay! It's miles away, and we don't know the way, and it is a wild forest, where people are savage and barbarous."

But she knew they could not go back—only on into the unknown country before them. Numb with cold, she eventually fell into an exhausted doze.

IV

Mistress Ladbrooke

WHEN the crying of the baby awakened Kate she saw that it was morning. The light filtered palely through dusty gratings high up the walls, and illuminated such festoons of cobwebs that she was glad she had not known they were there the night before. She felt unspeakably weary and cramped, but the baby's needs were far more urgent than hers. He was sitting up in her lap, and had been crying fretfully, but now that he saw that her eyes were open he stopped.

"You poor baby," said Kate. "I hope you will soon get something to eat." She looked at David, and saw that he was still fast asleep, and he looked very dirty and tired. Kate hated to wake him, but she decided that it was time. She shook his arm gently, and he opened his eyes with a mumbled protest, then sat up and looked about him. Kate couldn't help laughing at the comically rueful expression that came into his eyes as he realised where he was.

"Glory, I'm stiff!" he exclaimed, scrambling to his feet. "What is his Royal Highness crying for?"

"He's hungry, wet, and uncomfortable, poor lamb," said Kate; "so am I damp, incidentally."

"Damp?" queried David.

"So would you be, if you'd been nursing a baby all night," said Kate.

"Help!" exclaimed David. "This rather complicates matters, doesn't it? I wish he was a few years older."

"Well, he isn't," said Kate, "and he can't help it—can you, baby? We'll have to wash the things somehow."

"How on earth . . ." began David, but he was interrupted by the shrill whistle they now knew to be Tommy's.

"All right?" queried the familiar hoarse voice, and Tommy appeared on the stairs carrying a bundle wrapped up in a dirty old shirt. The children greeted him with relief.

"What about the Ladbrookes?" asked David.

"What's in the bundle?" clamoured Kate.

"Don't make such a din!" warned Tommy. "This warehouse is empty, but there's folks about not far off."

He opened the bundle, displaying proudly a can of milk, a loaf of bread, a meat patty, and some ragged old clothes.

"Thought mebbe you'd want some change for the baby," he said. "I'd two younger'n me, so I know," he added rather grimly.

Kate could have embraced him. Everything was far from clean and probably stolen, but she was not in a mood to be particular. She stripped off the gold bracelet that had long been her only trinket, and thrust it into Tommy's hands quickly, determined not to show the regret she felt at parting with it. He looked at it in awe for a moment, then tucked it away in some hiding place about his ragged person.

The three of them shared the patty and the baby had bread and milk.

"I ought to have some warm water to wash him," said Kate.

Tommy snorted scornfully.

"Wipe 'im," he said; "that's all our ma ever did."

Kate could well believe it, but she looked doubtful. David said impatiently, "Heavens, Kate, it'll have to stay dirty. We can't be fastidious now." He turned to Tommy again. "What about the Ladbrookes? Did you find out anything?"

"He's an apothecary," said Tommy; "lives in Bright Street—that's not very far from here. My pal George says he's a funny old stick and hasn't no use for the likes of us."

Kate looked doubtfully at her brother.

"Are you sure those are the people he meant?" she asked. "Dare we go to them?"

"We must," said David; "we can't possibly get to Tomay without their help."

"Tomay!" echoed Tommy, and whistled. "You ain't goin' there, surely? You'll never get there! Or if you do you'll get lost in the forest and die."

"We've got an uncle there," explained David; "we're going to him."

"Cor!" exclaimed Tommy. "What's he like? One o' my pals says all Tomayans are warlocks and robbers."

"We don't know what he's like," said Kate, and thought that for all they knew Uncle Hugh might indeed be a warlock or a robber—or even worse. Uncle Clarence had dropped dark hints. She looked desperately at David, who said firmly:

"He's our mother's brother, so he must be all right."

Tommy looked sceptical.

"Could you tell me how to get to Master Ladbrooke's house?" David went on to ask. "Kate, I think I'd better go alone, if you don't mind—I'll come straight back— but they may be searching for the two of us."

Kate nodded dumbly. She did not like to stay alone, but there was nothing else for it. On Tommy's advice David left his coat and stockings behind. Without them he looked hardly less of an urchin than his companion.

"You'll be cold," protested Kate.

"Can't be helped," said David; and the two boys went away up the stairs.

Left alone, Kate walked up and down with the baby, singing softly to send him asleep. She found that by knotting one of the shawls that Tommy had brought she could support his weight from her shoulders and rest her arms. He soon dropped off to sleep, being full of bread and milk. Kate looked down at his small face and thought it looked grimy and pathetic. She herself felt tired and drowsy and very cold. She decided that Tommy had been right. They had very little hope of ever reaching Tomay alive at this time of year. They were city-bred children used to an indoor life, and their only outings had been walks in the park with their cousin, and occasional drives in the carriage with their aunt.

Kate halted in a patch of dusty sunlight in sudden irresolution. Perhaps it would be better to go back, and to give up the baby. Perhaps Rupert Mountmaris of Craglands really meant him no harm, for after all they had only John Forester's word to go by. Supposing he had been kidnapping the baby for the benefit of the Prince of Tomay, who was the King's next heir? But then Mountmaris had announced the child's death when all the time he was alive. It was quite impossible to understand.

Slowly Kate pulled out the letter John Forester had given her. It was a thin packet addressed in a clerkly hand.

"To His Highness the Prince of Tomay, by the hand of John Forester, equerry to Her Late Majesty Queen Corinna."

She turned it over and studied the seal—a blob of scarlet wax that bore the uneven and, she felt, hasty impression of a signet ring.

A sound from the direction of the stairs made her put the letter away in haste and turn apprehensively to face the entrance. She breathed a sigh of relief as David came down, followed by a neat little grey-haired lady, who threw up her hands with an exclamation of pity as she saw Kate.

"This is Mistress Ladbrooke, Kate," explained David. "I have told her all our story, and I think you had better show her the letter that John Forester gave you."

Mistress Ladbrooke drew near, and Kate pulled out the letter without any misgivings. The little lady had such kind and honest eyes that it was impossible not to trust her. She took the letter in a small hand that trembled a little, and looked at the superscription and the seal.

"Ah," she exclaimed softly, "His Majesty's seal!"

"Is it?" cried Kate excitedly. "I thought so. A horse with a crown round its neck. I'd heard it was the royal seal. Then it is all right—I was beginning to think . . . to wonder . . ." she hesitated, flushing a little.

"John Forester is an honest man," said Mistress Ladbrooke. "I only hope he is all right now."

She took the baby from Kate and crooned over it.

"The darling!" she exclaimed. "Poor little mite!"

"Then if it is all true," said David, "why has Mountmaris announced that the baby is dead?"

Mistress Ladbrooke looked bewildered and distressed.

"I'm afraid he meant to kill him," she said. "And the poor King seems to be quite helpless. With Tomay out of the country there is no one to stop the Duke of Cragland's schemes. The White Guard are all powerful in the city now, and they are everywhere."

Kate shivered.

"The baby will never be safe, then," she said.

Mistress Ladbrooke gave the child back to Kate, and wrung her thin little hands together.

"Then you can help us to get him to Tomay?" asked David. "We cannot go back to our uncle and aunt now, and we have another uncle in Tomay who might help us."

Mistress Ladbrooke looked very worried.

"I do not know what to do," she said. "My husband would have known, but he is away, gone to visit his sister, and he will not be back for a week. Perhaps I could hide you in my house for a time while I send to him—yes, that would be best—and then my husband will know what to do."

"Oh, that would be very kind of you!" cried Kate gratefully, but David hesitated.

"I don't want to be discouraging," he said, "but I don't really think we should hang about for longer than we can help."

"But, David," protested Kate, "if we keep hidden we shall be quite safe."

"It's difficult to hide a baby," David pointed out; "they cry and attract attention."

"That's true." Mistress Ladbrooke seemed very agitated. "Oh dear, however shall we get you to Tomay? If only His Highness had not had to go to Mir, I'm sure this could never have happened. I think I must hide you until I can get in touch with my husband. I cannot possibly arrange the business myself!" She fluttered help-lessly. "You must come to my house."

"We cannot go in daylight," Kate pointed out.

"No, no, you are quite right," said Mistress Ladbrooke, "it would be folly. You must wait here until dark. What are your names?"

"David and Katherine Holt," said David.

"I will go back and fetch you a basket of food, you poor children," said the old lady. "What about the little beggar boy who guided you, David? Is he trustworthy?"

"We hardly know him," confessed David, "but we had to trust him, and he only thinks we are running away."

Mistress Ladbrooke shook her head anxiously.

"I don't like it," she said. "It's all so risky. Well, I'll go back and get you some provisions, and you must wait quietly till I return."

She hurried away up the stairs, holding her spotless grey skirts out of the dust.

"She is a nice old lady," said Kate, when she had gone. "I feel much happier now."

David was less sanguine.

"I wish her husband had been there," he said restlessly. "I feel she is muddled, and I don't like all this waiting about."

"It will be all right," Kate reassured him cheerfully. "I wonder what she will bring us to eat? I'm hungry again. Look, the baby is waking. I'm going to play with him."

So they settled down to await developments.

V

Captain Varek

"IF I have to stay here much longer," cried Kate suddenly, "I think I shall burst."

"Cheer up," David encouraged her. "It's nearly dark—and listen, I hear someone coming."

"It's not Mistress Ladbrooke!" whispered Kate in sudden fear. "It's someone running."

She was right. It was Tommy who pelted headlong down the stairs.

"You must move from here!" he gasped urgently. "They've been looking for you all over the town, and one of the gang saw me come down here this morning, and suspected. He's gone to report to the watch."

Kate hastily gathered up the baby, who was once again, mercifully, asleep.

"You haven't much time," went on Tommy. "And we'll have to go carefully, for they have been searching in this district, because you were seen here last night. Your uncle seems to have set the whole town by the ears!"

"He's a—he's a determined sort of person," explained David lamely. And then he asked helplessly, "Where can we go?"

"To the Ladbrookes, of course," said Kate, but David hesitated.

"I don't want to bring trouble on the old lady," he said.

"It seems to me there's more in this than meets the eye!" said Tommy dubiously.

"Oh, Tommy, there is, there is!" cried Kate. "But please believe in us! We are not doing anything wrong, truly we are not."

"Wouldn't care if you was," Tommy said gruffly. "You treated me square, and I wouldn't give you away. But I'm not so sure as I wants to go on with it."

"No, you mustn't," said David, with sudden determination. "There's no reason why you should become involved in this mess as well as us. I think you ought to go back to your gang, and go at once."

"I was thinking I'd lie low until all this had blown over," said Tommy. He paused, as though reluctant to leave them.

"Goodbye, Tommy," said David firmly. "And thank you for warning us."

"Goodbye," said Tommy, "and good luck!" Then he went, rather slowly.

David and Kate looked at each other.

"Oh, David," whispered Kate, "what have we started?"

"I don't know," answered her brother; "but we are at war, and they are at peace, and we ought not to drag peaceful people into our war."

42

"War!" exclaimed Kate. "What a war! The Protector, the White Guard, the watch, all against us, and no one for us, except poor little Mistress Ladbrooke. We shall have to go to her, David. There's no one else who will shelter us."

He nodded. "I don't like it, though," he said, his voice full of trouble.

It was nearly dark outside and all was very still except for the eerie crying of the seagulls as they flew up the river.

"That means stormy weather!" whispered Kate.

There was no one about, and their footsteps echoed on the stone wharf. The very silence was sinister, and Kate felt that every barrel and bollard must hide a spy. She had never been so afraid in all her life. Her heart was pounding violently, her mouth was dry, and her knees trembled.

David led the way into a small alley, where the poor tumbledown houses seemed to meet overhead. There were lights in the windows and some people about. Here and there dirty children played on doorsteps, and men slouched in corners talking. A dog was gnawing a bone in the gutter and growled at them as they passed.

Anything should have been comforting after that dreadful silence by the river, but Kate felt as though she was still moving in a bubble of terror. All these human, comforting sights and sounds were outside the shining, shaking walls of it. She and David and the little Prince were alone, entirely alone, in the populous city, and without hope of succour. It seemed to her that everyone stopped whatever they were doing to stare at them—

some with curiosity, some with resentment at the intrusion of "foreigners" into their own alley.

Kate was glad when they turned into a broader thoroughfare where the houses were larger, and merchants were busy closing up their shops for the night.

It was here that they heard the sound of hoofs, and someone cried:

"It's the White Guard!"

David dragged Kate up a small passage way between two houses, and there they crouched among the garbage piles, and watched a company of the dreaded horsemen clatter by. They rode at a jog, and carried torches that flared and sputtered, lighting up their stern faces as they glanced from side to side of the street. By the very entrance to the passage their leader drew rein and questioned a man. The children could hear his words, quite loud and clear.

"Fellow! you there! Have you seen two children, a boy and a girl, about thirteen and twelve years old?"

"No, I have not!" answered the man ungraciously, evidently resenting the questioner's tone. He had not noticed David and Kate, for he had been busy putting up the shutters of his shop.

But a small child piped up.

"I saw a boy and girl—just this minute! They went that way——" and he pointed unerringly at the mouth of David and Kate's passage way.

"Nobody asked you to speak!" screamed some woman, probably the little boy's mother, and the children saw her grab her offspring by the ear and drag him back.

"Always telling stories, he is!" she complained bitterly. "Don't you believe a word he says, your worship!"

The captain said gravely:

"His lordship the Protector would not take the word of a child, my good woman."

Then he rode on, his men following him.

"Bless the woman," whispered Kate, who was trembling all over. "They've gone away not knowing."

"I can hardly believe our luck," agreed David. "Come on, we'll get out this back way."

They went down the dark, evil-smelling passage, and came out into another street much like the last, and proceeded on their way unmolested.

"I think we're going vaguely in the right direction," said David more cheerfully, but Kate turned a blanched face to his.

"David," she said softly, "we're being followed. I saw a man come from the passage behind us—just out of the

45

tail of my eye, I saw him—and now we've been round three corners, and he's still there. Don't look round now, but as we cross to that corner you'll see him. He's wearing a black hat, and I don't like the look of him in the least."

David obeyed, and then said: "Yes, I see. We'll dodge a little and try to shake him off."

They slipped round a couple of corners, and down a back street, and at first they thought they had lost him, but as they came out into a spacious square there he was, still behind them, and Kate imagined she saw him smirk at her as she shot a terrified glance over her shoulder.

"We *must* keep where there are people," said David desperately. "I don't believe he'll do anything then. We must stick to these more busy streets and hope we shake him off. If not . . ."

Kate shivered. It was getting later and people would be going to bed. Already the streets were emptying. She did not like to think of what would happen if they were left alone with their pursuer in a deserted alley. She knew that by now David must be as hopelessly lost as she was. They would never find the Ladbrookes' house, even if they had dared to risk leading the man in the black hat thither.

"If only we could ask someone to help us," panted Kate, "or find somewhere to hide."

Then they turned a corner again and before them was an empty street—dark and very still. Kate gasped.

"In here!" David ordered.

There was a small stone chapel on their left, and it had a low, penthouse porch. Into this porch the two children scuttled, and crouched behind the heavy iron-studded door that stood ajar.

"He'll guess we're here," murmured Kate. Her arms were aching from the weight of the child, and she felt sick.

"Quiet!" whispered David, gripping her wrist.

They heard the steps of their pursuer come round the corner, then hesitate and grow slower. He had seen that the street was empty, and knew that they must be hidden somewhere. He was coming towards the chapel, slowly— slowly.

David was trying the chapel door behind them, but it was locked.

They were trapped.

Then, suddenly, they heard a shout, followed quickly by the rapid sound of running feet, for someone had come into the street at its other end and at the same time a shadow darkened the entrance of the porch. They saw the outline of the black hat.

"Do not move!" hissed a voice. "If you cry out, it will be the worse for you."

It was a quiet, cold voice, and David instantly hated it.

"Come from behind that door!" it ordered.

There was a shout of drunken laughter from up the street, followed by the clash of steel, as the two children came silently from behind the door.

The man in the black hat struck flint and tinder and lighted a lanthorn which he had carried under his cloak. This he stood on the bench which ran round the length of the porch.

"Ah!" he said, his eyes on the baby.

"No, no!" gasped Kate. She drew in her breath and shrieked louder than she had known she could, but her scream stopped abruptly in the middle as the man in the black hat threatened her with a fierce gesture.

"Foolish child!" he said sternly. "You may cry out, but do you think anybody will help you? They are too much engaged on their own private brawls, the drunken young blades! It will be better for the baby if you are quiet. Do you understand me?"

"Yes, sir," whispered David.

"Good." The man took off his black hat, and without it he looked rather less sinister, though there was that about his face which made them still distrust him.

"Now, children, listen to me," he went on in a more kindly tone. "You have been very much misled by this traitor, John Forester. It was foolish of you not to wake your uncle and aunt at once and let them deal with the situation."

Kate opened her mouth to speak, but shut it again, deciding to leave the talking to her brother.

"Sir," said David, "my uncle and aunt would only have been angry. We had to do what we could. John Forester told us——"

He paused, wondering if he had said too much.

"I can guess what he told you," said the man sternly. "Some cock and bull story about this child being the heir to the throne, was it not? Yes, I can see by your faces that I was right."

He gave a short laugh, and looked at them in smiling tolerance.

"I am Captain Varek," he said. "I expect your friend Mr. Forester may have painted a rather unpleasant picture of me. As it is, I am just a man like any other. I have children of my own. So has his lordship the Protector, my noble patron. We would neither of us be likely to dream of hurting a little child."

"No, sir," said David politely, "but——"

The captain raised a slender hand. The shouts of the brawlers were drawing nearer. One of them was singing a nostalgic tune to the broken chords of a lute, his clear tenor voice somewhat blurred by wine:

> "The river is wide, I cannot get o'er,
> And neither have I wings to fly—
> Bring me a boat that will carry two,
> And both shall row, my love and I . . ."

There was a shout of applause from one of his companions. The captain, who had frowned at the song, as though there was something about it, or the singer's voice, that displeased and puzzled him, then smiled crookedly and turned back to the children.

"This baby was the Prince's foster brother," he explained, "the Foresters' own child, who was born at about the same time as His Royal Highness the late Prince. Mistress Forester nursed the Prince with her own son, and when he died she and her husband plotted to substitute their child."

David, who had stood silently with bent head, now looked up and gazed steadily into his captor's eyes.

"It was a strange scheme for people as simple as the Foresters to think of," he said boldly.

"Ah"—Varek glanced from David to Kate and back again—"he is intelligent, your brother, my little mistress. Yes, I grant you that—but Forester was more subtle than he appeared. Besides, he had someone else behind him—someone who is a power in the land."

"Who?" demanded Kate swiftly.

The captain smiled a little.

"Shall I reveal state secrets to such children as you?" he asked. "This man is so powerful—he has insinuated himself to such an extent into the hearts of the people—that it is not yet safe to accuse him openly. It will take time and perseverance to make the people realize that they have been mistaken in their hero."

"Then he must be a great danger to the state," said David quietly.

"He is, indeed," agreed Varek. "His name—you see, children, I trust you—his name is Adrian St. Louis, Prince of Tomay."

"But——" began Kate, thoroughly bewildered. David interrupted her.

"We thank you for your confidence, sir," he said politely. "And I think we understand now. But there is one thing we should like to know. What is to become of this baby? You see, my sister has grown very fond of him."

"Oh yes, I have," Kate put in. "He is a darling."

David was playing for time, she knew. How splendidly he was acting! She was determined not to let him down.

"Oh, sir," she cried eagerly, "Mistress Forester and her husband will go to prison, I suppose? Well, please, couldn't I keep the baby?"

The captain smiled indulgently, but Kate thought she detected a flicker of impatience in his eye.

"You are too young, child, to take such a responsibility," he said. "I will take the little one, and his lordship the Protector will see that he is well cared for. You may have confidence in that. Surely your uncle has told you of his greatness?"

"Oh yes, sir, often," said Kate with truth.

Then the captain once again held up his hand for silence. The revellers were very close now. Some of them passed the chapel door, shouting a chorus. The lutanist crashed out a discord and they howled with laughter. Kate looked desperately at David, as their footsteps faded.

"Then you must trust me," Captain Varek was saying, and he held out his hands for the baby.

"I leaned my back against an oak,
Thinking to find a trusty tree!"

sang the mocking voice of the lutanist, very close.

Captain Varek whirled round, and they saw the man standing on the porch steps. He was steady on his feet for a drunkard, and they could see the white of the lace at his throat and wrists, and the long, gleaming blade of the naked rapier he held in his right hand.

Varek caught up the lanthorn from the bench and held it high. His other hand grasped Kate fiercely by the arm.

"You!" he exclaimed, and he swore, adding, "I thought you were abroad with your precious master!"

Kate whimpered. "Let go, you're hurting!" she said.

"Let go of the little girl, Varek," ordered the stranger.

"I will call the guard!" cried Varek. "What business have you to interfere, you red fox?" but he dropped Kate's arm.

"I have always had a liking for interfering in other

people's affairs," said the other impudently. "It seems to bring me luck. No, you don't!"

The captain had whipped a pistol from under his cloak, but before he could fire his arm was caught by the red-headed gallant. For a moment the two swayed together on the steps, and Kate was fearful of the result, for Captain Varek was a broad, heavy man, while his opponent was spare and slender; but by some trick the redhead wrenched the pistol from Varek's grasp and flung him off.

"Guard!" shouted the captain, even as he fell. They heard the sound of furiously galloping hoofs.

"Come!" ordered their rescuer, snatching the baby from Kate, and they found themselves running for dear life, the baby, who had been awakened by the noise, screaming frantically.

They pelted down a steep flight of steps, along an alley, then when Kate thought her heart would burst, they stopped under a high wall in a dark passage.

"For pity's sake make it stop!" The stranger fairly threw the baby at Kate. "If it won't I'll have to knock it on the head."

"Y–you were holding him upside down!" panted Kate indignantly as soon as she could speak. "Baby, it's all right! Ssh!"

Miraculously, the little Prince's shrieks subsided. The redhead had given David a leg up on to the top of the wall. He followed himself, then reached down to lift Kate and the baby. In a few minutes they were all on the other side, in a garden, where it was very quiet and peaceful, and the sounds of pursuit sounded faint and distant.

Their rescuer led them up a path between the trees. They crossed a wide lawn, and then came close under the walls of a great house.

"Where are we?" whispered Kate.

"Greenways House," answered the redhead in the same tone. Then he led them to a side door and knocked loudly three times.

VI

Greenways

THEY were kept waiting quite a long time before
they heard footsteps hurrying towards the door
on the other side. Then someone drew back the
bolts, and it opened a crack.

"Who is there?" asked a man's voice, with a soft,
broad accent unfamiliar to Kate and David.

"It's I, Sholto St. George," answered their rescuer.
"Let us in, Ned. I've got some children here, and they
seem to be dying on their feet."

Indeed, he was supporting Kate with his arm, for
fatigue had made her dizzy.

"Master Sholto! Come in, come in!" The door swung
wide open, and they saw a little man, scarcely taller than
David. He stood aside to let them pass, sheltering the
flame of his candle with one hand. Then Sholto St.
George shut and re-bolted the door.

"Mercy on us! What have we got here?" queried the
little man called Ned, who was brown and wizened and
very long in the arm, and wore curious clothes—a pair

of loose, shapeless breeches topped by a homespun shirt worn outside them and belted with a broad strip of leather. "The little lady looks weary. Here, little mistress."

He took the baby from her, and, carrying him as if he had done nothing else all his life, led the way up the passage and into a great kitchen where there was a blazing fire. Here they made Kate lie down on a cushioned settle and gave her something to drink that made her cough and splutter, but brought the colour back to her blanched cheeks.

"What is it?" she asked, as soon as she could speak.

"Brandy," said Sholto. "Feel better now?"

"Yes, but dreadfully sleepy," answered Kate.

"You're awake enough to drink some hot soup. There's some in the pot. Come along now."

Ned had ladled some steaming concoction into a bowl, and gave it to her as he spoke. She sipped it drowsily while Sholto and David sat down and were served in their turn.

While they were drinking their soup, the amazing little man called Ned departed with a warming-pan to air beds. Then he returned and attended to the baby, who was now grizzling sorrowfully. Deftly he washed him, fed him, and made him comfortable in a bed of rugs on the settle at Kate's feet.

Sholto seemed amused.

"Where did you learn to be a child's nurse, Ned?" he asked.

"I've had four of my own," grunted the little man. "The wife used to get fed up sometimes and turn them over to me."

"Where are they now?" asked Kate, who was beginning to recover a little.

"Grown up, miss, and living their own lives. The two girls are married and have children of their own, and the boys are working on their land as they should, and serving their Prince."

David sat up suddenly.

"What is this place?" he asked.

"This is Greenways House," replied Sholto. "It's His Highness the Prince of Tomay's town house. At present it is empty and Ned is acting as caretaker."

David and Kate exchanged startled looks.

"Please—" said David, "we thank you very much for helping us—but how did you come to—I mean——"

He hesitated, unable to put his question as he wished to. Sholto explained:

"I heard your sister scream; then when I was outside the chapel door I heard Varek's voice. As I've never known him do an honest thing yet, I decided to investigate. Then I heard him say, 'You must trust me,' and I felt called upon to give you a warning, for he's no man to trust. And now I'd like to ask you a question. How did you fall foul of him?"

David looked worried. "I don't know that we can explain," he said. "It's all so difficult. But we have to go to Tomay, and that quickly."

"To Tomay?" Sholto's keen blue eyes widened. "It's a long way."

"Not so far, not so far, Master Sholto," protested Ned. "With a good horse and a knowledge of the cross-country ways."

"Yes, but," Sholto pointed out, "they have no horse,

they have a baby to carry, and they have made an enemy of Varek. Incidentally, so have I! I shouldn't be surprised if a detachment of the White Guard didn't come to arrest me at any moment."

Ned's eyes flashed.

"In this house? They wouldn't dare!" he exclaimed.

"I'm not so sure," said Sholto. "Adrian of Tomay is far away, and Mountmaris seems to be supreme. His Majesty," he added with some scorn, "appears to have forgotten that he has a kingdom to govern."

"They say he is overcome with grief," put in Kate rather reproachfully.

"Well," Sholto changed the subject, "since you will not tell me how you have run foul of the Protector's shadow, perhaps you will deign to tell me your names?"

"We are David and Katharine Holt," answered David. "And"—he indicated the baby—"this is our little brother. We lived with an uncle and aunt and they took charge of us because our parents were dead, but they have always made us feel we were a nuisance to them, and we hated it, so we came away, and we are going to our other uncle in Tomay."

"I see," said Sholto. "Does this other uncle know that you are coming?"

"No," replied David, "but there is no one else to whom we can go."

"Hum!" Sholto looked keenly at him. "Have your parents been dead long?" he asked.

"Nine years," Kate said. Then, realizing what she had done she put her hand to her mouth in dismay.

"He's not very well grown, is he?" Sholto indicated the baby. "Are you kidnappers, or what?"

Kate, too tired and discouraged even to attempt to cover up her mistake, burst into tears.

"I couldn't help it!" she sobbed. "You caught me out. Oh, I can't bear it—every one laying traps. . . ."

"Kate, Kate, don't cry," exclaimed David in dismay, but Kate could not stop. She had been through a gruelling twenty-four hours, and now the reaction had inevitably come. Sholto St. George seemed discomfited at the storm he had roused, and Ned looked at him reproachfully.

"There, little mistress," he said soothingly. "What you want is sleep, and you can talk in the morning. You're quite safe here. Master Sholto would never betray you if you had kidnapped the Protector himself. He is no lover of Varek's—nor are any of us in this house; so you can rest in peace. You too, young master, come to bed."

"But what about the baby?" gulped Kate.

"You can take him with you," Ned reassured her. "I'll bring him along and we'll put him to bed safe and sound. Come along now."

They followed him out into a passage, and up a great stairway, at the top of which were two bedrooms next door to each other. Ned raised the candle he carried and showed Kate the great panelled room with tapestry hangings.

"Goodness!" she exclaimed, her voice still shaky from crying. "This is much too grand for me!"

Ned laughed. "Good night, mistress. Your brother is next door, so you need not feel lonely. And don't you feel afraid. Master Sholto's bark is worse than his bite."

He winked at her, and departed, leaving her the candle.

Kate made the baby comfortable, then, almost too tired to undress, tumbled into bed herself. She slept the deep sleep of complete exhaustion. David, in the next room, was not slow to follow her example, though he lay awake for a little while wondering what the future could hold in store for them.

He was half inclined to trust their new friends with the whole story, for he felt instinctively that they were honest; yet they were obviously friends and servants of the Prince of Tomay, who had cause enough to wish the little Prince out of the way, since he was the next heir to the throne. But then Varek, David remembered, had said that Tomay was at the back of the plot to substitute the Forester baby for the Prince. That had sounded quite fantastic. David had been ready to believe Varek until he had made that statement.

The boy determined to be wary and to suspect everyone until he had a more certain idea of the truth, but he was beginning to feel fairly sure that they had been right in the first place, and that John Forester was honest, and Varek a liar.

"I'll talk to Kate about it in the morning," he thought drowsily, and in a few minutes he was asleep.

When Kate awoke the next morning it was to hear the baby crying for his breakfast. She sat up and smiled sleepily at him and, to her delight, he stopped howling and held out his arms to her.

"You nice baby!" exclaimed Kate. "It's worth it to help you, even if you are not a Prince."

There was a knock at the door, and when she called out: "Come in!" Ned entered, carrying a tray, which he set down on a table near the bed.

"Your breakfasts, mistress," he announced. "I heard the baby crying and guessed he must be getting hungry. Squeal like little pigs to be fed, don't they?"

"Yes," Kate agreed. "What a wonderful breakfast! You are very good to us."

"It's nothing, mistress," said Ned. "I'll bring you a can of hot water afterwards to wash the child and yourself. Did you sleep through all the racket?"

"What racket?" asked Kate.

"Why, the Protector's men knocked us up in the small hours and demanded to know if Master Sholto St. George was here. They had an order to arrest him, and they also enquired if I had seen anything of two children and a baby."

"Oh dear!" gasped Kate, who had turned pale. "How terrible! Have they arrested him?"

"No, mistress. He was away from the house, and I told them so, though they didn't believe me. Then they demanded to search the house, but I would not let them do that."

"How could you stop them?" asked Kate.

"Why, they had no warrant, and I said that without a warrant signed by the King I could not allow them to search my master's property. After all, he is answerable to no one but His Majesty."

Kate stared at him soberly, sitting up in the great bed with the baby in her lap.

"I wonder they went away," she said.

Ned shrugged. "They will come back," he stated

grimly. "Master Sholto has gone to arrange for your journey into Tomay."

"But they may find him and arrest him!" cried Kate in a panic. "Oh, and all because of us! How dreadful! And they might arrest you, too, for refusing to let them search the house."

"I don't think they will." Ned shook his head. "Tomay would have something to say if they did, and he is on his way home, Master Sholto tells me. He's just come from Mir himself—some trouble among his own people in the Lud's Dale brought him back. They're in Mountmaris's Province and have been Scouting his authority. Now, mistress, eat your breakfast. I'll send your brother in to eat with you."

"Does he know about all this?" asked Kate.

"Yes, the noise they made woke him, and he came to the head of the stairs and heard it all."

"But what if they come again? Where shall we hide?"

"Your brother knows."

He disappeared, and in a few minutes David came in to breakfast. He was fully dressed, but looked untidy and sleepy.

"I slept in my clothes," he confessed. "Kate, I've made my room look as if no one had been in it. You'd better do the same, as soon as you've finished eating. Then we can disappear into the secret place Ned showed me without leaving a trace."

"What about that?" Kate indicated the clothes-basket in which Louis had spent the night.

"Take it with us."

It was difficult to be calm when any minute they might have to run and hide. Only Louis was quite unperturbed.

62

He dragged himself up by the edge of the clothes-basket and laughed at them over the top.

"Oh, look," cried Kate admiringly, "he's standing up!"

"Rubbish," scoffed David. "He's holding on to the edge. That's cheating."

Kate laughed.

They piled the plates on the tray, and David took it down to the kitchen, and came back with some hot water. Then Kate dressed herself and Louis and made the bed.

"I wish I could wash some clothes," she sighed. "But I daren't, for I fear we shouldn't have time to dry them."

As she spoke Ned knocked at the door again, and this time he produced, with the air of a conjurer, a pile of spotlessly clean baby clothes.

"Oh," cried Kate in delight, "wherever did those come from?"

Ned winked. "I'm a magician, I am," he said. "And now, master and mistress, I wish you, please, to stay in this room. If you hear anyone knocking on the door, Master David, you know what you must do."

David nodded.

"Yes, Ned," he said. "And we are most truly grateful to you. We quite realize that you are doing all this at great risk to yourself."

"In Tomay, Master David, there are laws of hospitality," replied Ned. "Besides, I am quite certain that my master, the Prince himself, would have helped you if he had been here."

David looked worried.

"I don't know about that," he said dubiously.

Ned grinned and left them.

Kate was dressing the baby in his new clothes. "He looks quite fine now!" she said.

David was not usually interested in babies, but he found, to his surprise, that he was getting fond of this one. He and Kate forgot their responsibilities and went down on their hands and knees and played with their charge.

"I suppose I ought really to put him to sleep," Kate said doubtfully, in the midst of an uproarious game.

"Oh, he's not a bit tired," protested David.

"Hush!" warned Kate suddenly. "What was that?"

They both sat up, listening intently. Then David opened the door a crack.

"I heard horses outside, and voices," whispered Kate.

Then, into the expectant silence, there burst a loud knocking on the door.

"Quick!" whispered David, seizing the clothes-basket, and bundling odds and ends into it. "Bring the baby and follow me."

Kate cast a last hasty glance into the empty room and saw that everything looked tidy. Then she hurried along the passage after her brother.

"Open," a harsh voice was shouting, "in the King's name!"

David was struggling with a heavy door at the end of the passage.

"This leads into the other wing of the house," he whispered, as he somehow got himself and the clothes-basket through it.

Kate followed him and closed it behind her, and it was

64

so thick that it shut out the voices of their pursuers and the knocking as well. As she looked round her she gasped.

"Oh, David, what a wonderful place!"

They were in a long gallery, with great high windows all along one side.

"Hurry, Kate," ordered David. "No time to admire it now. They may be through at any moment. Run!"

They ran up to the other end, and David opened a small, narrow door which led into a library.

"This is where I wanted to stop and admire," he said with a grin.

He went up to one of the shelves and took out a book.

"Templar's *Hawking and Venerie*, volume III," he said.

"What are you doing?" asked Kate, puzzled.

"You wait." David tucked the fat volume under his arm and inserted his hand into the gap it had left. Then, before Kate's astonished eyes, the whole of one section of the shelf, books and all, sank noiselessly back into the wall.

David replaced the volume and went through the gap with his clothes-basket. Kate followed with the baby, and David touched a spring which closed the entrance again.

"Well, what do you think of that?" his voice asked triumphantly out of the darkness.

"Marvellous!" exclaimed Kate. "But what happens if the baby cries?"

"Ned says the walls are so thick that only a really loud cry would be heard—but try to put him to sleep."

"He ought to be sleepy by now," said Kate. "Perhaps we'd better not talk so loud."

She sat down on the floor in the dark. It was stone and very cold, but it was easier to nurse the baby sitting down. She could now see a faint beam of light coming from a kind of ventilator high above their heads. The space they were in was very small.

"It feels very shut in," whispered Kate with a little shiver.

"Ned said there was another way out," said David. "Listen!"

Faintly they could here someone shouting.

"Oh dear!" whispered Kate. "I do hope Ned will be all right."

"I wish we knew that other way out," said David. "It would——" He stopped, for behind them, from the wall opposite the one they had come in by, they could hear a faint tapping.

66

"Oh!" gasped Kate.

"Rats," suggested David, but his voice trembled.

"It's not rats," said a faint, distant voice. "Stand right away, the two of you. This door opens towards you and there isn't much room."

It was Sholto St. George's voice. They could recognize it, muffled as it was. They stood as far as they could from his direction, and dragged the basket out of the way. Then there was a creaking sound, and a vertical crack of light split the darkness. It widened slowly as a wooden panel swung inwards towards them, and they saw Sholto standing in the gap at the top of a flight of steps. He had a lanthorn in his hand, and was no longer dressed as a gallant, but in clothes very similar to Ned's, only shabbier and older.

"It's time you were getting on the road to Tomay," he said. "Come!"

VII

Fugitives Away

T HEY followed him obediently down a steep wind-
ing staircase that seemed endless, and, at the
bottom, found themselves in a cellar.

"They've searched this part of the house," said Sholto
briefly. "You'll be quite safe, only you must keep quiet.
Wait here a minute while I go up and close the panel."

He disappeared, moving so quietly that they could not
hear his feet on the stone stairs. When he returned he
closed the door in the cellar wall and rolled an empty
barrel in front of it. So cunningly was it devised that
Kate blinked, and wondered whether there had ever
been a door there at all.

"We're very sorry," said David apologetically. "We
seem to have got you into a mess as well as ourselves."

"You certainly have," agreed Sholto, but there was
a twinkle in his eye, and he did not seem to be angry.

"We've been a nuisance to a lot of people," confessed Kate. "David, I wish we could get word to Mistress Ladbrooke that we are safe. She will be very worried
about us."

Sholto smiled. "She knows you are here," he said. "As it happens, she is an old friend of mine, and was very kind to me once. I went to see her last night, and found her nearly beside herself because you had not arrived."

"Oh!" exclaimed Kate. "You are a friend of hers! Then I'm sure it will be all right to tell you everything."

"Mistress Ladbrooke told me what she knew," said Sholto, "and I don't think we've time to stand talking now."

"No," agreed David, "but how are we going to get out? Surely the house is being watched?"

"The trouble with you two," said Sholto, amused, "is that you talk too much. Didn't your uncle ever squash you?"

"Frequently," replied Kate with a sigh.

"Well, you ought to be in practice. Be quiet at once and listen to me."

"Yes, sir," said David, and Kate tried to look intelligent.

"A friend of mine is a carter who brings fuel and food into the city, and takes home other goods. He has a covered wagon and he has agreed to help you to pass out of the city. He says he will arrange to hide you efficiently, which will be necessary as the cart may very likely be searched at the city gates. He will wait under the western wall of the garden at eleven o'clock—that is in about an hour's time. Our problem is to get you to it without being seen."

"Can't we get over the wall as we did last night?" suggested Kate.

"There is a door," said Sholto, "but it is daylight,

remember; although this cloudy weather may help us. It looks as though a rainstorm will break before long."

Kate glanced down at the baby, who was sleeping peacefully in her arms. Then she looked at Sholto.

"Will you come with us?" she asked.

He shook his head.

"I must stay in the city," he said, "and try to find out what has happened to the King, and to John and Lucy Forester."

"The King!" exclaimed David. "But nothing can have happened to him."

"I'm not so sure." Sholto shook his head. "Our heroic Duke of Craglands is not over scrupulous, and his secretary, Varek, is even less so."

There was a muffled knock on the cellar door, and Ned appeared, grinning all over his face.

"They've gone," he said. "And they were wild at finding nothing. Maybe they're afraid to return to my Lord Protector and confess their failure." He shook his head rather sadly as he added: "Things have come to a pretty pass. It might have been better if His Highness had stayed near the King—or at least in the country, where he was within call."

Sholto nodded gloomily. "But who was to know that Mountmaris would go as far as this?" he asked. "Well, when I left Mir Tomay was already finishing his work there and he should soon be on his way."

Ned brought the children down some food and urged them to eat well.

"It may be your last square meal for some time," he said. "So make the best of it."

Sholto had gone out to reconnoitre. When they were just finishing the last crumbs, he returned.

"They have posted watchers all around the place," he told them. "It's easy enough to tell what they are there for, though they wander about trying to look unconcerned. I shall make a rather obvious getaway, and that should draw them off. I want you to wait with Ned in the garden, close to the small door in the wall. Then, when I have gone I hope you'll hear the racket. Wait while you can count ten, then, if the coast is clear, slip out into the alley. Bill is there with his wagon. He has been tinkering with one of his horses' shoes, and talking with the watcher, as friendly as you please."

They followed Sholto out into the garden. It was raining now, steadily, and Kate and David were glad of their cloaks. They walked along a path between two high yew hedges, and saw the wall they had come over the night before, and in it a green door.

"Wait there," whispered Sholto. Then he took a running jump and vaulted on to the top of the wall. There was a shout, and the crack of a shot. Sholto ran along the top of the wall, and leapt on to the penthouse roof of an adjacent building. He seemed to be as agile as a monkey.

Kate and David had forgotten to count ten. They watched Sholto disappear over the top of the wet roof-tops, and heard the sound of running feet and shouting, and a couple more shots.

"Oh," exclaimed Kate, "he'll be killed!"

"Not he," answered Ned comfortably. "Come on, now."

He fitted a key in the well-oiled lock of the door and

turned it softly. Then he peered cautiously out into the street. It was empty, except for a heavy covered wagon to which were harnessed two huge draught horses. A man stood beside it staring open-mouthed after the pursuit.

"Come on now," said Ned, "in with you."

The wagoner nodded, suddenly ceasing to look stupid. The two children scrambled over the tailboard with Ned's help, and as the sacking that screened the back of the wagon dropped into place they found themselves in darkness.

"Goodbye," said Ned's voice, "and good luck to you."

"Goodbye," they answered softly, "and thank you for everything."

The baby stirred in Kate's arms. The wagoner spoke to the horses, and in a few minutes they were rumbling noisily over the cobblestones.

"One thanksgiving," Kate said in David's ear, "they won't be able to hear the baby through this if he chatters or cries."

The wagoner looked back at them with a kindly eye.

"Ye'd better hide yerselves," he told them. "Ye can hide in among the bedding that I'm taking for Mistress Fagan at the inn. It's likely they'll look inside when we come to the gate."

The bedding was in rolls and piles. There were feather beds and mattresses and bolts of cloth.

"Come on, Kate," said David. "I'll roll you and the baby up in one of those mattresses."

The baby yelled vociferously at this indignity, but eventually both he and Kate were safely concealed.

David made a cocoon for himself out of a feather bed. In a few minutes, when Louis had consented to be quiet, you would not have known that there were three children in the wagon.

They stayed thus for what seemed hours to Kate. She was unbearably hot, and she was sure that the baby could not breathe properly. Then the wagoner pulled up his horses, and they heard a voice demand:

"What have you got in there, fellow?"

"Bedding, and cloth, yer honour," replied the wagoner. "It is for my sister-in-law that keeps a house in Perigal."

"I'll just take a look."

They felt the wagon rock as he climbed over the tail-board. Someone drove a sword into the mattress that concealed Kate. It shook, and the blade grazed her arm. Louis opened his mouth to cry. Kate put her hand over it. She could not help it if she hurt him. She knew he must not make a sound.

"All right, carry on," said the voice. She could hardly believe it. The wagoner cracked his whip and the equipage trundled on. Kate held tight for a moment before she released the child, and the shriek he gave then was the weaker because the poor little thing was half suffocated. Kate expected that someone would have heard, and that they would be stopped again, but no, on they went, and very soon David was thankfully unwinding her.

It was not very comfortable, even when they could sit on the feather beds. The roads were bad, and there were no springs in the wagon, which rocked crazily in and out of the ruts. The rain beat down on the canvas roof above them, and soon they began to grow cold, and had to wrap themselves in the feather beds and quilts to keep warm. As soon as they were warm again they began to feel hungry, and Louis started to cry for his tea.

Now and again the wagoner, who told them his name was Bill Fagan, looked back at them to see how they were getting on.

"When shall we be at Tomay?" Kate asked him once. He roared with laughter.

"It's two days' journey from Ree City to Tomay. Keep going at this speed," he said. "And almost a day to the edge of the forest. But I'm only taking you to Perigal. That's near to the Tomay border, and once you're over it you'll be well looked after. There'll be something arranged to take you on."

Kate's heart sank. The shaking was beginning to make her feel sick. David, who was unaffected by it, took the baby from her and amused him by singing to him until he fell asleep. He tried to remember the song Sholto had sung.

"I leaned my back up against an oak,
    Thinking to find a trusty tree——"

To his surprise the wagoner took up the song with a lusty bellow.

"But first he bended, and then he broke,
    So did my own true love to me!"

So they rolled on along the muddy road through the pouring rain, and by and by the dusk began to gather, and Bill Fagan suggested that the children should come and sit up beside him.

"There's not many folks here," he said. "And we're nearly in Perigal."

The rain had stopped, and the evening star had risen over a clump of sparse pines. Far ahead of them they could see the winking lights of a village. Bill pointed with his whip.

"Perigal," he said.

VIII

The Golden Apple

Iᴺ Perigal the children were taken to the hostelry
called The Golden Apple, which was kept by Bill
Fagan's sister-in-law, a stout, rather formidable-
looking widow. When Bill told her that the children were
fugitives from the Protector, she looked taken aback,
and asked what they had done to incur his displeasure.

"I don't know," Bill said rather crossly. "I didn't ask.
I helped them to oblige a friend of mine."

"Huh!" The widow put her arms akimbo, "I know
your friends! Come forward, children, and speak for
yourselves."

They came and stood in the full light of the lanthorn
that hung in the porch.

"We're extremely sorry," said David politely, and he
added: "If we are inconveniencing you we'll go somewhere else."

At that the stout lady suddenly relented.

"Come inside, young gentleman, and you, mistress,"
she said more gently, "and warm yourselves by the fire
while I get you some supper."

David hesitated. "I'm afraid we've no money to pay for anything," he said.

"That's all taken care of," Bill reassured him, and mistress Fagan broke in with: "Bless your hearts, it wouldn't matter anyway!"

Bill went away to untack the horses, and the children followed Mistress Fagan into a big kitchen, where a maid whom she addressed as Margery was busy at the sink. The two women at once snatched the baby from Kate and began to croon at him. He resented this deeply, and screamed until they handed him back.

"He's very fond of you," said Mistress Fagan. "Is he your little brother?"

Kate was tired of telling lies and being caught out, so she answered, "No."

"Have you run away with him, you wicked children?" cried their hostess, with a disconcerting change of front. "Oh, his poor mother!"

"His mother is dead," explained David, and he added, "Truly, we have not done anything wicked—at least I don't think so. We are going to our uncle in Tomay."

"But how have you managed to offend the Lord Protector?" asked the puzzled hostess. "Of course I can see you are not wicked children—a nice little lady and gentleman like you—but I can't help being worried. You see, this house has a good reputation, and I shouldn't like it to be spoilt."

"We should hate to bring trouble upon you," said David earnestly, "and if it can be arranged we will go on our way this very night. Perhaps the money for our night's lodging could be used for transport?"

"No, no, my dear, I wouldn't dream of that," protested Mistress Fagan. "You both look weary, and should have a night's rest. We won't say any more about it, and you shall sample our cooking."

But she still looked worried, and more than once during the evening they saw her whispering to Bill, with many glances in their direction, but he appeared to give only monosyllabic replies.

When they had eaten an excellent supper, the children were hustled to bed. Mistress Fagan herself took a candle, and showed them where they were to sleep.

She lifted her candle with some pride and let its flickering light illumine the proportions of the lofty rooms.

"Nothing poky about my house," she said. "The King himself could lie here in comfort."

"The King!" exclaimed David involuntarily. "I wonder what he is thinking now?"

Mistress Fagan looked at him curiously.

"His Majesty is the guest of his lordship the Protector at Perigal Castle," she said. "Just up at the top of the hill."

Kate's arms tightened round the baby.

David paled. "You mean," he faltered, "that the Protector is in Perigal—and the King?"

"Yes, young man, I do mean it," she replied. "His lordship the Protector was granted the castle of Perigal as a gift from the King, and he often comes here. This time he has brought His Majesty with him. They say," she went on with a sympathetic sigh, "that the King was so deeply afflicted by Her Majesty's death that he is very ill. It is hoped that the good air of Perigal will hasten his recovery."

"I hope it will," agreed Kate doubtfully.

A clatter of hoofs outside made them all look up sharply.

"It's just someone passing along the street," said Mistress Fagan, but she went to the window and peered out between the curtains. Standing just beside her, Kate saw a detachment of the White Guard ride up the village street. Some of them carried torches, and in the raw glare of these their uniforms looked red.

"Fine they look, don't they?" Mistress Fagan said admiringly. Kate shivered.

Weary as they were, it was a long time before the children could sleep. It seemed to them that wherever they went the Protector's power dogged them.

"I wonder," thought Kate, "whether Captain Varek is here?" She did not express her fears to David, because he seemed tranquil and confident. Had she known it, beneath his quietness he was feeling as worried and miserable as she was herself. It was almost uncanny the way things had gone against them. But weary minds cannot chase round in circles for ever, and they slept at last, to be awakened before dawn by Bill, who had crept up to their room in his bare feet, leaving the clogs he usually wore downstairs.

"What is it?" Kate asked, alarmed.

Bill put a finger to his lips and indicated that she must dress at once. David had been roused too, and was more wide awake than she. They bundled into their clothes, and Kate went to pick up the baby. He was still asleep in the wooden cradle Mistress Fagan had lent them.

"Don't you make him holler!" cautioned Bill in a hissing whisper. "Here, I'll take the cradle and all."

He lifted the thing as easily as if it had weighed nothing, and carried it carefully down the stairs. The children followed silently.

There was a woman standing in the kitchen. She was tall and gaudily dressed with iron-grey hair and a copper-coloured face. She wore gold rings in her ears and her brilliant eyes looked very fierce. Kate, who had never been so close to a gipsy before, but had heard many stories about the wicked things they did, shrank back behind Bill.

The wagoner shut the door at the foot of the stairs and spoke in a low voice:

"This is Jane Rider. She brings you a message from Sholto St. George."

The woman grinned at them, and her white teeth gleamed in her dark face. She thrust a grimy hand under her scarlet shawl, and drew out a crumpled letter, which she handed to David.

David turned it over. There was no superscription, but the seal was there, a curious one, with a bold impression of St. George on horseback, braced on his spear, which passed out of the picture to transfix an invisible dragon. David broke it and unfolded the letter, which was brief, saying as follows:

"You can trust Jane Rider absolutely. Give the Prince into her charge and take the horses Bill will give you and ride north into Tomay to find your uncle. I would come myself, only if I risk showing my face in Perigal at present it may endanger you more. Destroy this letter.
                              "Sholto St. George."

David showed the letter to Kate, who flung herself in front of the child, and cried, "No, no! I will not give him to her!"

The gipsy woman was silent, her dark eyes inscrutable.

"You had better do what he says, mistress," advised Bill, "and that quickly. It is nearly sunrise, and the whole of the province is being searched for two children and a baby. He will be far safer with her, and you can move more freely."

"Yes, Kate," said David, also siding against her. "He is almost certain to be captured if we take him with us. It is best to obey orders."

Kate wept. She remembered the stories of gipsies who stole and murdered little children.

"No, no," she stammered through her tears. "I won't let him go. He cannot have meant it."

"I will not hurt him, little lady," Jane Rider spoke at last, in a deep, husky voice with a strange lilt to it. "Have I not brought up six fine sons of my own? I will care for this little one as if he was one of those."

Perhaps it was her voice, or her compelling dark eyes that made Kate give way. Louis had woken up and was grizzling fretfully. Jane Rider took a swift stride forward and picked him up. In her arms, tucked in the shawl, he was quiet.

"You see," the woman crooned. "He is all right with me."

"I suppose so," sobbed Kate. "But where will you take him? He looks very white beside you."

"A little walnut juice and no one will ask any questions," answered the gipsy. "I will take him up to

Tomay for you with our people. You will find us at Fleet, by the spring, where we camp every year."

Bill opened the door for her and she slipped out into the dim morning. Kate, who had stopped crying, felt lost and giddy, and her courage had all left her. Bill and David tried to cheer her, but she drooped, and longed suddenly to be out of it all, and safely back in her aunt's Ree City house.

"Never mind," Bill reassured David, "she will be all right with a good mount under her and on the road to Tomay."

"But I cannot ride," protested Kate.

Bill looked blank.

David said: "It's true. The stable boy taught me a little on the carriage horses, but Kate never learned. Our aunt didn't think it becoming for a girl."

Bill stared at such heresy.

"Well," he said, "she will have a side saddle, and she can be lashed to the pommel. She will have to learn as she goes."

Kate thought them very unsympathetic. The steed she found waiting for her in the yard was only a forest pony, but she felt much too high up on it, and very insecure, in spite of the rope Bill tied round her.

"We ought to say thank-you to Mistress Fagan," David said, as Bill gave him a leg-up.

"I'll say it for you," answered Bill. "I put something in their posset," he added with a grin, "to make her and Margery sleep late. Keep straight on the road and then fork left. Anyone will tell you the way."

He looked after them anxiously. Both looked very insecure on horseback, and their disappearing figures were pathetic.

"Poor little devils," murmured Bill. "Perhaps I should have gone with them?"

"It was just as well you didn't, my man," said a voice at his elbow. "Just as well. . . ."

Bill turned, to see a gentleman in black standing beside him.

"Sir?" he gasped. "You came up so quietly you startled me."

"Where is the child?" demanded the gentleman.

"What child?" Bill assumed his stupid expression.

The gentleman blew a little whistle and four men in the uniform of the White Guard came round the house.

"You, Royland and Smith," ordered Captain Varek—for he it was—"ride after those children and bring them back. Sergeant Timms—arrest this man! We will take him for questioning after we have searched the house."

"Oh, no you don't!" shouted Bill in sudden fury. He charged Varek himself, bowling him over, and scattered the astonished troopers by the very force of his attack. He was round the corner of the house and out of sight before they had time to gather themselves together sufficiently to draw their weapons and fire a few wild shots after him.

"Wouldn't have thought the yokel had it in him!" commented the sergeant, as he helped the swearing officer to his feet.

IX

Kate Delivers the Letter

THE troopers Royland and Smith did not hurry after the children, since they knew they had them at their mercy.

"They may have no baby with them," Royland pointed out to his companion, "and they may lead us to him. The captain would reward us well if we brought him that baby."

"Yes," replied Smith thoughtfully. "I wonder why?" Royland shrugged.

"It's not our place to ask questions," he said. "The Lord Protector demands unquestioning service. If we give him that he will advance us."

"Yes," agreed Smith, but he looked dubious.

The two children, intent on the serious business of riding, did not notice that they were being followed. David was enjoying himself. His pony felt narrow and bouncy after the sluggish old carriage horse he had started to learn on. Even Kate, who was very uncomfortable and nervous, found that the fresh air and unaccustomed exercise drove her giddiness away.

It was David who looked behind him first and saw the two troopers just topping the hill. He gave a soft exclamation, and Kate too twisted round in her saddle.

"Oh," she gasped, "whatever shall we do?"

"We shall have to run for it," announced David. "In those woods ahead we might be able to lose them. We'll take this bridle path which goes in the direction of the trees, and see if they leave the main road to follow. After all, they may not be following us. We shall soon see."

He turned on to the bridle path and urged his pony into a trot. Kate's followed, and she bumped miserably, till she felt the jarring would loosen every tooth in her head.

"Oh, David, need we?" she gasped.

"We must," he answered. "Try to rise, as I do."

He demonstrated, not very expertly. He had only had a few lessons in trotting. Kate tried, but the cords that tied her bit into her waist painfully. She turned round again and saw that the two troopers had broken into a canter and followed them on to the bridle path, as if they did not want to lose their quarry in the woods.

"They're coming this way—much faster!" gasped Kate.

"Then we must gallop," said David.

David had never cantered, far less galloped. He reached up and pulled a stick from a hazel bush, and hit his pony. It leapt forward, and with a cry he over-balanced and fell in a heap at the side of the path. The pony, now thoroughly frightened, shot off at full speed, with Kate's following it.

"Oh, David! Stop! Stop!" shrieked Kate, but her cries only frightened the ponies more, and the terrible pressure of the cords that bound her to the saddle soon made her concentrate on holding on to the mane, the pommel, anything that would take her weight off them. She had no time to look back and see if her brother was hurt before they plunged into the wood and tore headlong along the ride. Terrified that the branch of a tree might put an abrupt end to her career, Kate crouched low and closed her eyes.

Then, quite suddenly, a voice called out, "Woa there!" and miraculously she felt her pony slow down and at last stand still, blowing hard.

At first she hardly dared to open her eyes to see what new danger threatened, but she looked up, shrinking.

She saw a man on a great bay horse. To her relief he was not wearing the uniform of the White Guard, nor even the apparel of a gentleman, but was dressed like Sholto and Ned, in a peasant's shirt and breeches.

She watched him, too frightened to speak, while he dismounted, leaving his horse to stand by itself, and came across unhurriedly to her.

"Who tied you on like this?" he asked.

Kate could not answer. She was feeling very sick.

The stranger busied himself with Bill's knots. When he had loosened the cord he lifted Kate down, and she swayed, hardly able to stand.

"Don't be afraid," he said, "I'm not going to hurt you."

"My brother!—" Kate managed to say, "he fell off, back there—oh," she exclaimed, as there was a thudding of hoofs, and Trooper Royland burst upon them, having left his comrade Smith in charge of David. He pulled up his horse, looking rather taken aback.

"Mistress," he said to Kate, "you must come with me."

Kate was about to submit, but the stranger demanded: "Why must she go?"

"It is the Lord Protector's order," replied Royland. "Stand out of the way, you!"

He made to come forward belligerently, but something unyielding in the stranger's aspect made him stop in mid-stride.

"What have you done?" her rescuer asked Kate. "Are you such a dangerous criminal?"

"Oh no," answered Kate, "but I had better go. They have got my brother back there. He fell off the pony, and he may be hurt. Besides, I don't really want to be separated from him."

"In that case," said the stranger to Royland, "show me a warrant, and the young lady may go with you."

"I have no warrant," replied Royland hardily. "His lordship the Protector has dispensed with such formalities long since."

The stranger's lips tightened.

"Has he indeed?" he queried. "I have been away too long, I think, and am behind the times. I'm afraid my ways are old-fashioned, for I regret to say that I shall not allow you to take a prisoner from here without a warrant."

"Some paltry peasant farmer, I suppose," sneered Royland. "I see it is true, what I have heard about Tomayan conceit. Well, then, if you will not give her up I must take her by force."

The stranger thrust Kate behind him as he whipped out his rapier. Royland had also drawn his, and, spurring his horse, bore down on his antagonist. Their blades clashed a moment, then the stranger thrust swiftly under Royland's guard, and the trooper reeled in his saddle, clutching his shoulder, while his weapon dropped from nerveless fingers.

"The devil!" he exclaimed. "What sort of farmer are you?"

"Go back to your master," said the stranger, "and tell him that Tomay is old-fashioned enough to require a signed warrant for the arrest of any fugitive who has sought sanctuary on his land."

"Tomay!" gasped Royland, understanding dawning in his white face. With an oath he wheeled his horse and galloped away down the path.

"But what about David?" asked Kate anxiously. "I ought to go back to him."

"You could not possibly help him if you were a prisoner yourself," pointed out her rescuer.

"I don't know what I can do," said Kate; "and now you are in trouble too, through helping me. I do thank you very much, but I almost wish you hadn't."

"Don't do that"—he was adjusting the saddle on her pony, and looked round with a smile in his dark eyes—"for wishing never did anyone any good. Besides, how do you know I was trying to help you? After all, I have good reason to dislike Craglands' sending troopers to arrest children on my land without warrants. That is going a little too far, Protector or no Protector."

Kate felt suddenly light-headed.

"Then," she asked, "are we in Tomay now?"

He nodded.

"Then you are the Prince of Tomay?"

"At your service."

"I've got a letter for you," said Kate at once. She fished it out and gave it to him. "There was a baby, too," she explained.

"A baby?" He paused in the act of breaking the seal, looking puzzled. "What baby?"

"Jane Rider has him now," said Kate. "You'll see about it in the letter."

He broke the seal with an expression of comical bewilderment, but as he read his face grew grave. Kate watched him anxiously, though she no longer had any fears about his loyalty. Something told her he was trustworthy.

"What is your name?" he asked her when he had finished reading.

"Kate Holt," she told him.

"Well, Kate, we will ride to a farm where you can rest safely, and as we go you can tell me how you came by this letter."

"Not ride!" Kate shrank back, as he led forward the pony. "I—I can't really. I was tied on because I didn't know how."

He did not laugh at her, but there was a twinkle in his eye as he mounted his own horse and lifted her up in front of him.

"Fiddle has carried two before," he said, "and although he is an old horse now, I think he can manage your light weight for a little way."

He led the ponies one on each side, and they started up the ride merrily. Kate hid her face at first, then, as she gained confidence in the steadying arm of her companion, she began to enjoy the feel of their swift movement.

"Now tell me," he demanded, when he had slowed to a walk.

Rather jerkily she told him the whole story, from the moment when she and David had heard the baby crying in the night.

"I did not like to let him go with the gipsy," she ended, "but it seems that it is just as well that I did."

"He will be safe with Jane Rider," Adrian of Tomay reassured her. "Don't you worry about him. It is the King who is in trouble now, and your brother David. I wonder what Sholto is up to?"

"Do you think David will be all right?" asked Kate anxiously.

"I'm certain of it," he answered cheerfully. "They can only keep him prisoner. Don't worry, Kate, everything will be all right."

They came out of the trees as he spoke, and before them was a long, low farmhouse with clustered outbuildings.

"There was one thing I meant to ask you," the Prince said as they rode towards these. "What was your uncle's name—the one in Tomay, I mean? We can make inquiries about him."

"His name is Hugh Winter," replied Kate.

"Hugh Winter?" echoed Tomay. "He is an old friend of mine, and we will get in touch with him at once."

A man had come running to meet them, followed by a woman.

"Your Highness! This is an honour!"

Kate, utterly weary, but somehow much more tranquil in her mind, allowed herself to be fed and fussed over by the farmer's wife, Mrs. Verey, who was evidently acquainted with her uncle.

"What a surprise for Master Hugh!" she kept exclaiming. "What a surprise!"

X

David is a Prisoner

WHEN David fell off his pony on to the grassy ride he was shaken, but not hurt. Almost at once, before he could even scramble to his feet, the troopers' horses were upon him. They pulled up abruptly.

"You attend to him!" called one of them. "I'll follow the girl."

So Trooper Smith dismounted. David made a dive for the undergrowth, but he was grabbed and hauled back.

"Come on, now, none of that!" said his captor gruffly. "You come back with me. Your sister will be joining you in a few minutes."

He was lifted on to Smith's horse, and rode drearily back to Perigal in front of the trooper, past Mistress Fagan's house, and on up the hill towards the castle.

"Shall I be put in prison?" he ventured to ask.

"Don't ask me," Smith said. "Captain Varek will decide what is to be done with you, no doubt."

Captain Varek! David gave a little shiver, and sighed with relief because the baby Prince was safe.

94

"They can't do much with Kate and me," he thought. "What use are we to them? Probably they'll send us back to Uncle Clarence."

A clatter of hoofs behind them announced the arrival of Royland. He was grey-faced, and swayed in the saddle, clutching his shoulder, where his white uniform was stained red.

"The devil! What has happened?" cried Smith. "Where is the girl?"

"Escaped, damn her!" exclaimed his colleague. "But I've a piece of news that will make the captain sit up. Do you know who pinked me?"

"Some lawless Tomayan farmer," hazarded Smith, "who took the girl's part, I suppose."

"You're wrong, my friend," answered Royland. "No

farmer could worst me. It was Tomay, I tell you! Tomay himself! He has come back."

David could have shouted with triumph. Then Kate could deliver the letter, and she would be safe for the time being, at any rate. He had only himself to worry about.

They rode into the courtyard, and Captain Varek met them.

"What has happened?" he snapped. "Where is the girl?"

As Smith told the whole story David had the satisfaction of watching the gallant captain's yellowish face turn yellower than ever.

"All right," he said, when the report was finished. "Shut that boy up."

His self-control was admirable. He stood calmly while David was led away, and only the restless fear in his eyes betrayed his agitation. David was locked in a small room with a high, barred window, and left alone to meditate on his ill-fortune.

The castle at Perigal had been built in medieval times to defend the loyal province of Southland Royal against the raids made by bands of outlaws from the Tomay forest. It was a forbidding grey stone fortress whose later lords had done very little to make it more comfortable. The Duke of Craglands, its present owner, used it seldom, but was now in residence, David gathered from Trooper Smith, who locked him up.

The boy made the best of his poor quarters, and passed the time in thinking, singing, and making up rhymes, until Smith appeared with some dinner for him.

"You'd best make a good meal while you can," he announced gloomily. "His lordship will be sending for you after he has dined."

"Perhaps he will be in a good mood after his dinner," suggested David hopefully. "I hope his cook's genius was burning today."

The trooper grunted that David was cheeky, and went away, leaving the plate of food and a pewter mug of water behind him.

The food was reasonably good, and David was hungry —too hungry for his appetite to be spoiled by any nervousness about his fate. He made a good meal, then lay down on the narrow pallet to await developments; but he did not have to wait long, for Smith soon returned.

"Come along," he ordered David, taking his arm, "and mind you behave respectfully and answer the questions his lordship asks you, or it will be the worse for you."

David accompanied him meekly along a stone passage, up some stairs and into another passage, whose walls and floor were hidden by hangings and a carpet. In spite of this veneer of comfort, the atmosphere of the place was cold and damp, reminding David suddenly of the empty warehouse where he and Kate had spent such an unpleasant night. It was rather dark, too, because the infrequent windows were nothing but narrow slits set deep in the thick walls, and all of them were barred—it would be a difficult place to escape from, David decided.

They came at last to a heavy oak door, and went through it into a large and lofty chamber, which, though luxuriously furnished, had the same chill atmosphere as the passage. Captain Varek was standing near a table in the centre of the room, at which was seated a richly dressed gentleman whom David guessed must be the Protector himself.

The Duke of Craglands was then in the prime of

life, a tall, handsome man who dressed magnificently and knew how to make the best of his striking appearance. He was fair-haired, with a ruddy countenance, which might have appeared open and frank if there had not been a cold, calculating look in his blue eyes, while his mouth was hard and humourless.

However, he evidently meant to be pleasant to his young prisoner, for he said, not unkindly:

"Well, young man, and what have you got to say for yourself?"

"Nothing," answered David, with the most innocent air that he could muster. "My sister and I were going into Tomay to find our uncle."

The Protector rose to his feet. He was very tall, and towered over the boy, while Captain Varek hovered near his elbow, like a jackal by a tiger, David could not help thinking.

"Boy," said the Protector sternly, "it is useless to lie to me. I know that a certain traitor, one John Forester, entrusted you with a child, leading you to believe that you were rescuing the heir to the throne from my clutches. You and your sister brought this child to Perigal—that I know. I do not blame you for what you have done, although it was very foolish of you to undertake such an escapade. You were misled and influenced by clever and unscrupulous people."

His voice was not unfriendly, but it had a quality which David disliked intensely—a sort of toneless loudness. Kate watched people's faces when making her judgments about them, but David was more influenced by their voices. He answered politely:

"No doubt we were very misguided, my lord."

"You have caused trouble to a great many people by your folly," went on the Protector severely, "not least to yourselves—for your sister, it now appears, has fallen into the hands of the Prince of Tomay, who is a very dangerous and ambitious man."

"I am sure he will not hurt her," said David; "after all, she has done him no harm."

The Protector made an impatient gesture.

"She can be rescued," he continued; "he can be made to give her up. You can both be released and returned to the care of your worthy and generous uncle and aunt and we need say no more about this unfortunate and foolish affair."

"You are very merciful, my lord," said David, "but Kate and I would rather go to our uncle in Tomay."

"Well, that might be arranged," assented the Duke cordially, "but first, this child must be found. Where is he?"

David thought: "This is it!" The question had been put almost casually, but Mountmaris's pale blue eyes were on him like gimlets.

"I do not know where he is," the boy replied, and, literally, it was true.

"Come, you must mend your memory." The Duke's manner was almost jocular, but his smile was without mirth.

"I cannot tell you, sir," David persisted quietly. "I do not know where the child has been taken."

"My lord," Captain Varek broke in, "it seems to me that you are being too merciful. What this boy needs is a little discipline. I explained the situation to him and his sister in Ree City, but they were stubborn, and would not believe me. I think it is time the young rebel was taught a lesson."

"You may be right, Varek, you may be right," Mountmaris said. "Time will show." And he added, addressing David, "You will remain a prisoner, young man, until you can tell me what I want to know. I think you may find confinement rather tedious. . . ." He paused, interrupted by the sound of voices from outside.

Trooper Smith seemed to be protesting against the entrance of someone very persistent. Suddenly the door swung open, and a lady stood on the threshold, pausing there only a second before coming into the room.

"I am so sorry if I have interrupted you, your grace," she said. She spoke with a distinct foreign accent, and her manner was gay rather than apologetic. "But I was in a slight difficulty, as one of my horses has lost a shoe, and I was sure you would help me."

"Your Highness." The Protector turned to meet her, plainly endeavouring to conceal his annoyance as he bowed politely. "Of course I am always at your service."

The lady smiled charmingly and gave him her hand, then she turned unexpectedly towards David.

"Surely this is not your son, my lord? He has grown enormously."

"No, this is not my son." The Protector's face had gone brick red with annoyance. The lady's eyes sparkled, and her mouth shaped a soundless "Oh!"

Mountmaris continued reluctantly: "This is a lad that I have to chastize for playing a fool's trick. Bow to Her Highness the Princess of Tomay, boy."

David bowed over the hand she gave him without taking his eyes from her face. He thought he had never seen anybody quite so lovely. In her blue travelling dress she seemed to bring the light of the summer sky into that sombre room.

"May I plead that his punishment may be light?" she begged the Lord Protector, laughing.

"Certainly, if you wish it," replied Mountmaris, with stiff gallantry, and went on to say, with studied casualness: "Is His Highness travelling with you? I was not aware you had returned from Mir."

"No," she answered, "he went by way of the city because he wished to wait upon His Majesty. But now I find His Majesty is here, so it was all to no purpose. However, I dare say Adrian will overtake us, for he travels fast when he is alone. Perhaps, in the meantime, I might pay my respects to His Majesty?"

"Madame, I am very sorry," the Lord Protector's face grew grave. "His Majesty, as you may have heard, was very much upset by the deaths of our late Queen and the little Prince. His grief has made him very ill, and he can see no one."

"I am sorry," said the Princess simply, her face serious and concerned. "Perhaps you will convey our sympathy to him? I wish I could have spoken to him."

She sighed, and bit her lip. Then she glanced again at David, who was looking at her rather desperately. There were a great many things he wanted to blurt out there and then. He would have liked to have cried out that the little Prince was alive, that he believed the King was virtually a prisoner, but common sense made him hold his tongue. Mountmaris, suddenly making an effort to be cordial, began to offer the lady refreshments, to regret the absence of his wife, and to apologize for the bareness of the castle. David watched him conduct her from the room, and as she went, she smiled over her shoulder, a reassuring smile, which David felt was meant for him.

As the door closed behind them Captain Varek gave a long sigh, then smiled, but it was not a very real smile.

"Boy," he said to David, "you were wise not to speak—very wise. If you had it would have been sad for you—and for her!" He went to the door and called Smith.

"Take the boy away," he ordered. "The Lord Protector will send for him when he wants him." He turned grimly to David. "And you would do well to mend your memory," he said.

XI

Kate Meets a Princess

MISTRESS Verey set a large dinner before Kate and stood over her while she ate it.

"Don't you be worrying yourself about that brother of yours," she said, for Kate had told her some of her troubles. "You may be sure that Tomay will have him safe in less time than it takes to tell, and that the Duke of Craglands won't dare to harm him in the meantime."

"It's Captain Varek I'm afraid of," Kate confessed. "If they were going to . . ." she stopped, not liking to say anything about the threat to the baby Prince. Luckily Mistress Verey was so busy thinking about Kate's immediate welfare that she asked no questions.

"Your gown is very crushed and dirty," she said. "I'll find you some of my daughter's outgrown clothes."

She bustled away, to return with a pile of neatly folded clothes. Kate looked at them, politely trying to conceal her surprise.

"They're not like the ones you've been wearing,"

explained Mrs. Verey. "These are country clothes. They're what you'll wear if you've come to live in the forest."

She fetched a tub, set it in front of the kitchen fire, and then half-filled it with warm water from the huge black kettle on the hob.

"The men won't be in for a while," she said. "You can give yourself a good scrub."

So Kate scrubbed herself all over and then put on the queer clothes. There was an embroidered blouse of coarse linen, and a red wool skirt, wide and full, but not reaching to her ankles. Over the blouse went a black-velvet laced bodice, and over that again a warm woollen jacket. Kate felt a bit embarrassed at showing so much leg, and was glad of the warm woollen stockings. On her feet she had light scarlet clogs that were difficult to walk in because they were too big.

She was trying to unravel the tangles in her hair, which had not been properly combed for weeks, when the Prince of Tomay returned that evening with Master Verey. The farmer, like his overlord, was very tall, and Kate felt rather intimidated by their size.

"Why, Kate, you are quite a country girl now!" Tomay teased her.

"Not with such pale cheeks, sir," protested Master Verey. "But we'll soon grow roses in them."

"Please, sir," said Kate earnestly, addressing the Prince, and remembering to curtsey, "have you any news of my brother David?"

"He was taken into the castle and is a prisoner there," answered Tomay, "as is also His Majesty the King—Bill Fagan escaped and took to the woods."

"I wonder how far Mountmaris will dare to go when he knows you are back, sir?" speculated Farmer Verey. Kate stole an interested glance at him through a curtain of hair. On the rare occasions when she and David had gone to stay in the country near the city with their Aunt Marion and their Cousin Fanny, men like this farmer had been expected to bow their heads and touch their forelocks at frequent intervals when they were speaking to Aunt Marion, and here was Farmer Verey talking respectfully, but without a sign of servile humility, to a great nobleman. Kate had yet to learn that the Tomay farmers and foresters were a proud and independent people who considered themselves far above all city dwellers. To their Prince only they gave homage, according to the ancient tradition, but even to him they would not bow and scrape. He valued their loyalty all the more because it was not tainted with flattery, for he had learnt the quality of it during the struggle against the invader years ago, when he had led them in an almost superhuman effort to throw off the Uralian yoke. In those days Adrian St. Louis of Tomay had been a ruthless and daring leader, taking his life in his hands, and expecting, and getting, the same service from his followers, but now he was learning to rule his people with a light hand, and to wield temperately the power of life and death that he held over them.

Kate was amused rather than offended, as her Cousin Fanny most certainly would have been, that the farmer and his wife had accepted her, a young lady from Ree City, as their equal, if not their inferior.

"So much for your conceit, my girl," she told herself, wrestling with a particularly obstinate tangle.

She tried to listen to the talk of the two men, thinking it must bear on David's predicament, as indeed it did, but she found it difficult to follow. They talked of people and places that she did not know, and were evidently making plans to raise the warlike foresters.

"Civil war?" queried Farmer Verey at one point.

"It mustn't come to that," said the Prince decidedly. "We will keep our movements secret until we can get the King himself free."

The sound of wheels interrupted them, and Verey flung open the door, to reveal a coach drawn by four black horses rattling crazily along the rutty track. The coachman pulled up in front of the farm, and the two men, followed by an inquisitive Kate, went out. Farmer Verey hurried to the horses' heads while the Prince of Tomay opened the carriage door. A lady appeared on the step, laughing, put her hands in his and jumped lightly down on to the grass.

"I protest that these roads are beyond a joke!" she cried as she raised her face to kiss the Prince. "I have been swung about until I am on the verge of sea-sickness."

"Poor Joanna!" he teased her. "You will be wishing yourself back in more civilized parts."

"Ah, never!" She looked about her at the surrounding trees, and the beautiful old farmhouse with appreciative eyes. Mistress Verey had come hurrying out.

"Welcome home, Your Highness!" she cried. "You will be glad to come in and rest, my lady, and you must be hungry."

The Princess thanked her, then turned to the watching child.

"And this must be Kate," she said, smiling at Kate, who was instantly her slave.

"Are you a witch, Joanna?" queried the Prince. "How did you know about Kate?"

"Why, I met Sholto just outside Perigal, and he told me the whole story. Then I went to the Duke of Craglands with a tale of a lame horse—Sholto had loosened the off-wheeler's shoe."

"You actually went into the castle, madame?" asked Farmer Verey, who had left the horses to two of his hands. "That might have been dangerous."

She shook her head. "I don't think he has decided on open war yet. He admitted to the King's presence there, but said he was too ill to see me. I saw your brother, Kate."

"Oh, madame," cried Kate eagerly, "was he all right? Not hurt by his fall?"

"He looked very well, Kate, I promise you—not even greatly concerned at his predicament."

"That's good news," said Adrian of Tomay, as they went into the house. "And I'd wager a good deal that the King is not so ill as they make out. Do you know where Sholto is now, Joanna?"

"He stayed in Perigal to try and get information about the whereabouts of the prisoners and the possibility of rescuing them," answered Joanna. "Adrian, we ought to get that baby from Jane Rider as soon as possible."

"He will be as safe with her as anywhere," he said.

Joanna looked a little worried.

"I don't know—these gipsies are hardy folk, and the child has been delicately cared for. I should like to take him to the keep, where he can be with our own children."

"Oh, please let us fetch him," cried Kate earnestly. "Jane Rider looked such a—such a terrifying person. I was frightened of her myself, and she is going to dye him brown. Supposing it never washed off? Or supposing she really stole him, as they say gipsies do steal children. . . ."

Overcome with anxiety about her precious baby, Kate found to her horror that she was crying.

"Don't worry, Kate, it will be all right. Jane Rider is as trustworthy as you or I," the Prince tried to reassure her. "And if you and Joanna both think so, we will fetch him as soon as it is safe to do so."

"Oh, don't cry, Kate," Joanna soothed her. "It was so brave of you to have done all that you have done."

It was a novel experience for Kate to have anyone but

David caring whether she cried or not. Aunt Marion had been wont to call her outbursts tantrums and lock her in her room till she had "got over" them.

"Oh dear," she gasped, as soon as she could speak, "you are so kind, and that makes it harder to stop."

Joanna smiled. "Then perhaps it is good for you to go on," she suggested.

"If sympathy is no good, shall we try ferocity?" offered Adrian helpfully.

Kate hastily dried her eyes. "I'm all right now," she said.

Mistress Verey had come in with a tray. Princess Joanna had her supper, trying to persuade Kate to have a second one with her, and then afterwards, when her husband had gone out again, she finished doing Kate's hair, combing out the tangles with practised skill, and then braiding it as she said girls in Tomay wore it.

"I don't think you should do it for me," protested Kate shyly, "you are a great lady."

Joanna laughed. "I have been a great many things, Kate," she said. "I was a lady's maid once, and now I have a little girl of my own who has plenty of tangles in her hair. So you see I am quite an expert with a comb— in fact I rather like it—if the people sit still."

"I'll try not to wriggle," promised Kate. "Do tell me about your little girl. She can't be as old as I am, surely?"

"Anne is three," Joanna told her, "and one of the naughtiest children I ever knew, bless her! She takes after her father. Her brother is not nearly so terrible. He's five. Sometimes I think he should have been the girl and she the boy." She sighed, adding: "I haven't seen them for several months. Dear me, it seems like years."

"They must miss you," Kate said, thinking how lovely it must be to have Joanna for a mother. "Who is looking after them?"

"There are plenty of people at the keep to take care of them," Joanna said, "but mostly it's Judith. She's their nurse, and a dragon, but they adore her. Sometimes I'm quite jealous of her. But tell me about yourself, Kate."

"Do you really want to know?"

"Yes, indeed I do."

So Kate told her about Aunt Marion and Uncle Clarence and the trying monotony of life in Ree City, and about the escape with the baby. Joanna did not say much, but Kate could see by her eyes that she understood a great deal, and when she said good night she gave Kate a kiss which was somehow comforting.

"She understands what it is like to be lonely and miserable," Kate thought, as she curled up in her truckle bed, and, feeling much reassured, fell asleep.

XII

David Finds a Friend

DAVID awoke after his first night in Perigal Castle with mixed feelings. The Princess of Tomay's visit had somehow given him confidence, but at the same time he felt that it had disturbed Varek and the Protector. He had an uneasy feeling that they would spare no pains now to make him tell them all he knew about the whereabouts of the baby, and so it proved. As soon as he had eaten the rather frugal breakfast they brought him Smith appeared.

"I'm to bring you to His Excellency," he announced gruffly.

David mischievously asked after his friend Royland.

"Oh, he's grousing like a bear." Smith grinned suddenly, looking rather more human than he had hitherto. "But he was not very badly hurt. Come along now."

He was kind, in his rather gruff way, but seemed concerned that there should be no delay. He hurried David along the cold corridor to the room in which he had been interviewed before. This time the Protector was not there, but Captain Varek sat at the table looking even more sinister than usual.

"Good morning, my boy," he said, showing his teeth in what was meant to be a smile. "I trust you passed a good night?"

"Tolerable, thank you, sir," answered David, hoping he did not sound as frightened as he felt.

"Ah," said Captain Varek, sitting back comfortably in his chair. "Then perhaps your memory has mended a little?"

"No, sir, I am afraid it hasn't," replied David.

"Boy"—Captain Varek leant forward, and gripped the edge of the table—"this is a very foolish attitude. Believe me, you are quite out of your depth and by your own folly may bring down on your head consequences more unpleasant than you think possible. It is not for children to meddle in the affairs of adults. You would do best to obey me at once, and tell me what you know."

"But, sir"—David tried to assume an expression of innocence—"I cannot conceive what you can want me to tell you."

"Where is the Forester baby?" asked Varek directly.

"I do not know," answered David. "I told you that before," he added, rather plaintively.

Varek gnawed his lip. He was evidently feeling sorely tried, but he was a persevering man.

"Perhaps your life has been a little humdrum up till now," he said, "in the care of your good uncle and aunt. Perhaps you and your sister thought that this 'adventure' of taking a baby to Tomay would provide a little pleasant excitement—eh? But I assure you, my dear boy, that if you persist in this stubborn attitude, you will be heartily wishing yourself out of the whole business—and your sister."

"I believe she is safe," said David, with more confidence than he felt.

Varek jerked back again suddenly, looking at David from under lowered lids.

"That makes me suspect that you are less ignorant dupes than willing conspirators," he said, "or how should you believe that Tomay would protect your sister?"

David was taken off his guard by this sudden change of front.

"I—I have no real reason to believe that she is safe," he stammered, "but she had a——" He stopped himself, horrified.

The captain leapt to his feet and came round the table to him.

"She had what?" he hissed. "What did she have? You'd better tell me——"

"I won't!" gasped David, trembling from head to foot.

"Let no one ever talk to me about the innocence of children!" raged the captain. "His Excellency shall know of this—and I predict that it will be the worse for you, and your precious sister when we find her."

He indicated with a fierce gesture that Smith should take the prisoner away.

"Now you've got yourself into a nice mess," remarked that gentleman, as he conducted David to his room. "You may well snivel."

David swallowed his tears, hating himself, and struggled to look defiant.

"It was just that he gave me such a jump," he excused himself, "suddenly coming round the table like that."

Smith did not lock the door at once. He stood there on the threshold, hesitant, for a moment. Then, quite suddenly, he came into the room, closing the door behind him.

"I don't like this business," he muttered in a low voice, "ill-treating children—it isn't Christian. And what do they want that baby for?"

David's heart leapt with hope.

"Oh," he whispered, "will you help me? Will you? Will you?" He was almost crying again with relief.

"Hush!" warned Smith. "I can't say—I don't know, I'm sure." He seemed irresolute and troubled. "But I'll think about it. Now I must go. If they find me talking to you they'll suspect something."

He went quickly, and David heard him lock the door.

He could not settle down to pass the time in singing and dreaming, because he knew now for certain what he had only dimly realized before, that the Protector and Varek were entirely unscrupulous. He stood in their way, and he would be used as they wished to use him, then tossed aside or ridden down. His life, his individuality, meant nothing to them, except in so far as his defiance was an irritation to them. Tortured by his hopes and fears, he walked up and down until he was giddy, and then made himself sit on the bed until the cold chilled him through and through, then up he would get and walk again, and so on all through the long morning.

When Smith brought him his dinner he said desperately:

"Couldn't I have a book to read, or something?"

Smith shook his head.

"You're lucky to get any dinner. Varek was for starving you into submission. He may get his way yet."

He put the plate and a mug of water down on the floor, since there was no table, and closed the door quietly.

"You are not the only prisoner," he whispered. "I've discovered something. The King is also a prisoner."

"I thought as much!" exclaimed David eagerly. "Tell me, where is he?"

"In a tower room in the north turret. It is given out that he is so ill as to be out of his mind, and only Captain Varek's personal servant—a devil if ever there was one—attends to him. But this morning this fellow was off on some other errand, and since I have a good record they sent me instead."

"And the King?"

"Is no more out of his mind than I am, I'm sure of that, though he looks ill, I grant you. . . ."

"Did he say anything to you?"

"Yes, directly he saw me he started to fire questions at me. Who was I? Was the Protector in residence? What had happened to John Forester? Of course I preserved a wooden face and did not answer him."

David ate while he listened, thinking desperately.

Smith went on: "I don't want to meddle in this. I'm just a soldier, and it is my business to obey my superiors; but I don't like it. I'm not disloyal to the King."

"You'll help us," insisted David. "If they send you to the King again, will you give him a message?"

"What is it?"

116

David hesitated, looking seriously at the trooper. His face looked honest enough, but David was painfully conscious that he had had very little experience to train his judgment of men. Still, not much harm could be done, since things couldn't be much worse than they were already.

"Tell him," he said carefully, "that the baby is safe, and that I believe his letter has been delivered."

Smith repeated the message.

"And can you ever get out at all?" asked David.

"Sometimes. Why? Do you want to make contact with someone outside?" asked Smith uneasily. "I don't know that I can do that."

"If you could see Bill Fagan, at the hostelry called the Golden Apple," suggested David tentatively, "they might get word to Sholto St. George."

"That hostelry is being watched," said Smith. "I'd have to be very careful. We tried to arrest Bill Fagan, but he escaped. Still, I know his sister-in-law, the hostess at the inn, and I might get a message to him through her."

"It's difficult, but do try," begged David. "So much depends on it."

Smith gathered up the plate and mug and went away looking troubled and preoccupied.

"I don't know that I can do anything," he said as he departed.

David was left wondering whether he had said too much. To pass the time he tried to remember all the poems that his tutor had ever made him learn by heart. He was declaiming dramatically, striding up and down to keep warm, when the door opened again to admit not

Smith, but Royland, who looked rather sour and had one arm in a sling.

"Come along," he said, "you're wanted."

David dared not enquire what had happened to Smith. All kinds of terrifying possibilities flitted through his mind as, with Royland's good hand heavily on his collar, he walked dejectedly whither he was guided.

This time they did not go to the familiar room where David had endured his previous interviews, but turned right, went up some stairs, and along a different passage. Royland knocked at a door, outside which another guard stood as sentry. A voice ordered them to enter, and in they went.

It was a luxuriously appointed chamber, and a fire burned in the hearth. David, who was blue with cold, longed to draw near to it, and hold out his stiffened hands to the blaze, but Royland kept a hand on his collar, and made him face the Protector, who sat in a great carved chair with his long legs stretched out before him.

"Boy," said Mountmaris sternly, "I find that you have not been honest with me. It appears that you have a knowledge of this affair which you have hitherto concealed from me. I am a moderate man, however, and I intend to give you one more chance."

David did not speak. There was no sense now in being polite, or in feigning innocence.

"You are to tell me what has happened to the child that you and your sister kidnapped, and what your sister had to give to the Prince of Tomay—to be frank with me, in fact, about this whole affair. I give you until tomorrow morning to make up your mind. If you are not prepared to make a clean breast of it by then I shall have to treat your sister and yourself not as misguided children, but as my enemies, and as enemies of Prosperito. For"—and he drew himself up, his eyes blazing with pride—"I am Prosperito."

Then David said a thing he would not have believed it possible for him, a mere boy, to say. He told Kate

afterwards, rather shamefacedly, that perhaps it was the blood of his ancestors speaking in him.

"My lord," he heard his own voice say quietly, as he looked into the nobleman's eyes, "that is treason."

The Duke's face became slowly suffused with red. Then the colour ebbed, leaving it blotchily pale. His cold eyes blazed, and for a moment David wanted to shrink, fearing a blow.

"Take the boy away," the Protector ordered thickly, at last.

Outside, Royland shook David.

"You've cooked your goose now all right." He speeded David over the threshold of his prison with an ungentle boot and slammed the door.

"Till tomorrow," David thought. His own temerity still amazed him, but curiously, he did not regret it.

"It is true," he told himself fiercely. "He is a traitor. What was everybody thinking of to let someone like that have so much power? It must never happen again."

And he resolved there and then that he must never allow it to happen. This resolution seemed to blind him to the possibility of his imminent death, and made the night less agonizing than it might have been.

The Escape from Perigal

I<small>T</small> was too cold to sleep. David's room was built on a corner, with two outside walls, and throughout the night the wind howled with increasing fierceness. The boy had only one threadbare blanket, and no matter how he wrapped it round him, it seemed to let in a draught somewhere. Once, after a brief, restless doze, he awoke to find his teeth chattering and got out of bed to walk about in the darkness in an effort to warm himself. So severe was the cold that he found that all his faculties were concentrated upon it to the exclusion of everything else, however fatal and important.

"If only I could get warm! What shall I do to get warm?" It was the only thing he could think of.

At night, with the wind blowing like this and rattling everything, and the rain driving against the windows and the stone walls, the castle was full of strange noises, but David was not, like Kate, afraid of ghosts. He paid little attention to the noises until he heard a slight sound which seemed to be at his very door—a footstep.

David felt colder, if possible, than he had before. Could they be sending someone to murder him quietly? Surely not—his information would still be valuable to them.

The door swung inwards silently, and he could just distinguish a black bulk against the dimness of the passage outside. A voice whispered hoarsely:

"You there, boy? It's me, Smith."

David crept forward eagerly.

"Here I am," he whispered. "Did you deliver my message to His Majesty?"

Smith grunted assent.

"He looked a different man," he added, "after I had told him. And now you are to follow me."

David could hardly believe his ears.

"Escape?" he gasped, trembling with excitement. Smith grabbed his arm, drew him out into the passage and silently closed the door after them. They hurried along the corridor, David so excited that he could hardly breathe. He could feel Smith trembling, though whether from fear or excitement he did not know. They climbed a steep flight of worn stone steps and came out on to the roof, where there was a terrace above the battlements, and as David came through the trap door the wind almost knocked him flat. In the face of it he could hardly breathe, and the rain stung his cheeks. He turned his back to it, putting his hands over his ears to keep out the cold blast, but then Smith pulled his sleeve and motioned him to follow. They threaded their way between the chimney pots, and then David saw, standing against the battlements, two men, one cloaked and rather huddled, the other an erect, wiry figure that David thought he knew even in the darkness.

"Hullo, David." It was Sholto St. George, of course. "You all right? They haven't been pumping you too hard?"

David shook his head, his teeth chattering.

"They hadn't really started, but I think they were just going to."

The cloaked figure moved with a gesture of disgust.

"You're cold," said Sholto, feeling David's hands. "You'll never climb down the rope with hands like lumps of ice. I've got horses down the hill, but we've to climb out first."

He chafed the boy's hands as he spoke.

"Have my cloak," suggested the other man. "You go first, St. George, and I will follow you," he added stiffly to the latter, "if that suits your plan."

"It suits well enough, sir," replied Sholto briskly. He swung over the side, and started to lower himself down the knotted rope between two buttresses, walking the wall with his feet. Every now and then a gust of wind would buffet him against the great buttress on his left, but he clung like a limpet, and at last reached the bottom.

"Now, Your Majesty," whispered Smith softly. David looked up quickly, as he watched the King climb slowly over the battlement. He moved closer, his hand on Smith's arm.

"He'll never make it," he whispered.

They leant over the battlement and watched the King's slow progress down the rope. Sholto, hanging with all his weight on the end of it, tried to steady it, and mercifully the wind had abated a little, but the King seemed to the watchers above to move incredibly slowly until the end, when he descended with a rush, as though the strength of his arms was giving out.

"Now, you," Smith told David. "Over you go."

At any other time David would have been terrified by that perilous descent and unable even to begin it, but, remembering what awaited him in the castle, he decided that it was the lesser of two evils, took off the cloak, and swung himself over. His hands were still so numb with cold that they could hardly hold the wet rope, and as he lowered himself slowly from knot to knot the wind drove the rain in sheets against his body, plastering his clothes to him.

He thought: "I won't look down, and I won't let go," but he knew that at any moment his fingers, rendered nerveless by the cold, might loosen and drop him into oblivion. Once he lost his grip enough to slide far too rapidly from one knot to another, but somehow he saved himself, and hung trembling in mid-air.

"Come on," he heard Sholto's voice. "Get a move on. Smith's waiting at the top."

That made David pull himself together. He came down, and felt himself caught and put on his feet.

"It's the cold," he muttered, "I couldn't hold the rope—I couldn't. . . ."

"Well, hold it now, to help steady it for Smith," ordered Sholto. David obeyed silently, though his knees were knocking together from reaction. He realized afterwards that his light weight could not have done much good. Sholto was simply keeping him occupied so that he would not have time to collapse. Smith came down easily, hand over hand.

"Do we have to leave the rope here, for everyone to see?" he asked.

"No time to move it. They'll have to know. This way!"

As they hurried after Sholto, half blinded by the wind and rain and stumbling over the rough ground, they heard shouts in the castle behind them, and then the alarm bell, pealing out into the stormy night once—twice—then silence.

Sholto chuckled. "The Protector soon nipped that in the bud," he said, as he unhitched four horses from the tree where he had tied them. "He wouldn't want the villagers to know who was escaping. Mount, sir, we've no time to lose."

The King mounted stiffly. Smith followed suit, then Sholto gave David a leg up and swung on to his fidgeting chestnut.

"Hold on to that neck-strap like grim death," he advised David. "I've heard something of your prowess as a horseman. I'll lead him, so don't bother about anything except staying on."

David nodded, gritting his teeth and clinging to the neck-strap, as he felt the horse spring away beneath him. The night whirled past, the wind rushing in his ears. Sholto glanced round at him with an encouraging grin and called out, "All right?" And he nodded, breathless, exhilarated. They galloped down the hill, all four horses abreast, Sholto's red mare fretting to outpace the others. He talked to her: "Steady, Juniper, steady, old girl."

The dawn was just breaking behind the castle, the sky was pale grey. Looking back, David saw a group of horsemen like white ghosts detach themselves from the darkness of the building and start down the hill after them.

"We're being followed!" he gasped.

Sholto turned his head, drawing rein a little. Then he looked ahead at the distant forest.

"Ride your hardest!" he cried, and Juniper shot ahead, David's horse pounding along to keep up.

In the glorious excitement of speed such as he had never experienced before, David almost forgot that they were being chased. The track down which he and Kate had come on that unlucky morning flew past, and every time they looked back the pursuers appeared less close. Sholto, David noticed, was holding his mare in a little to keep her level with the rest of them.

"It's lucky the light's so bad," cried Smith, who was a little behind, "or there'd be shooting, not a doubt."

"We want to be well into the forest before it's much lighter," assented Sholto.

In a few minutes they were in the woods, splashing along a muddy ride. Sholto waved the King and Smith ahead, and rode on their heels. Blobs of mud splashed up at David until he was plastered from head to foot. The rain had slackened, but the wind bent the trees above their heads with its fierce gusts.

Suddenly as they rounded a bend, they came on a fallen tree across the way. Smith shouted, "Hup!" and his horse and the King's rose together and cleared it.

"Hold tight and lean forward!" cried Sholto, steadying Juniper so that she and David's horse were dead level. David saw the great tree-trunk ahead, gasped at the sight of it and clung to the neck-strap. He felt something rise under him and then, as he said to Kate later, it was all over

in a moment, and he found himself hanging round his horse's neck, clutching the neck-strap, the mane—anything. Some one grabbed his belt and hauled him back into the saddle. It was Sholto, and he was laughing.

"Help!" exclaimed David, struggling to regain his lost stirrups.

Sholto shouted to Smith then, and they slowed down.

"I'm going off the path," he said. "Follow me in single file, and keep your heads down, every one, and look out for branches."

They walked their horses carefully through the bushes, then trotted, twisting and turning through the thick woods, the horses picking their way with almost uncanny surefootedness. Sholto went first, then the King, then David, off the leading rein now, but still clinging to the neck-strap, and Smith came last.

"Surely that tree will stop them," said David.

"We got over it, didn't we?" growled Smith. "Don't talk so much."

Out of the wood on the moor they cantered again, and then entered a beechwood with great trees stretching up like the pillars of a cathedral. Here Sholto paused, and letting Juniper's reins go stood up on her back and swung himself into the branches of a tree. He climbed up to the very top, which seemed to sway dangerously in the wind, and looked around.

"There's no sign of them crossing the moor," he said, when he had come down. "I think we have shaken them off. We'll go steadily now, but we won't talk and we'll keep listening for the beat of their hoofs."

So they rode through the beechwood at a sober pace for what seemed to David an endless way, until, on the edge of another stretch of moorland, they came to a barn, where Sholto suggested they should dismount and rest themselves for a little while.

David slid thankfully to the ground, and discovered that he could hardly walk. Smith and Sholto laughed at him, and even the King smiled.

"I'm on the stiff side too," he confessed.

"You didn't do so badly," Sholto told David, his bright blue eyes so approving that David flushed with pardonable pride.

They went into the barn, horses and all, and sat down out of the wind to consume food and wine which Sholto produced from his saddle bag. There was a bale of hay for the horses in the barn which had evidently been prepared for their coming, and Sholto and Smith gave the tired beasts a rub down.

"They deserve better fare," grumbled the former, "but we can't be fussy."

David had the impression that Sholto had little liking for the King, whom he seemed barely to treat with respect. The King himself was stiff and gloomy for the most part. David felt unaccountably sorry for him. He found himself telling about John Forester's coming, and about his and Kate's journey with the baby. His Majesty's rather dulled eyes lighted up a little as he listened, and his long, pale face flushed slightly.

"You will not find me ungrateful," he said with haughty sincerity, and added rather bitterly, "through my own fault I have been helpless in this business, and have earned the contempt of my subjects. In fact"—and here he looked straight at Sholto,—"sometimes I hardly think they consider themselves my subjects."

Sholto reddened. "Sir," he said, "I never considered myself the subject of Mountmaris, or of any of Your Majesty's less scrupulous advisers. But now that you stand alone I will endeavour to prove myself loyal."

The King bit his lip. "I am very much your debtor," he muttered, and then fell moodily silent.

David felt embarrassed, and so, plainly, did Smith, who was not used to finding himself in such exalted company. He rose with relief when Sholto suggested that they should go on, although David, who had had to rest lying on his stomach, groaned dismally at the thought of the saddle.

"Cheer up," Sholto encouraged him. "It isn't far."

So they set off again. The wind had dropped a little and the rain had steadied to a monotonous driving drizzle, fine and very wetting. David, chafed and miserable and covered with mud, prayed for the journey through that endless and inhospitable forest to end.

XIV

Uncle Hugh

WHETHER the meal they had eaten at the barn was supposed to be breakfast or lunch, David was never quite certain. The day was so wet and dreary that it was impossible to guess at the time by looking at the sun. However, after a time the rain stopped and the sky lightened, although poor David was by then far too miserable to appreciate the improvement.

"Are there no houses in these parts," he asked Sholto, "where we could rest a little and get dry?"

Sholto laughed. "There are houses," he said, "here and there. But we have taken the ways which avoided them. Never mind, David, we are nearly at our destination, if you can bear to torture yourself a little longer."

"You won't get any sympathy from him, boy," said the King with a ghost of a smile, "he who's been climbing on and off horses ever since he could walk! I don't suppose he knows what it is to feel as you do now."

They came suddenly upon a clearing in the woodland, where there was a minute cottage with a garden beside it, a paddock, and a strip of cultivated land which looked too overshadowed by trees to grow anything. Just now it was stubble left by a sparse crop of oats, and an old man was ploughing it in with a primitive plough drawn by a diminutive farm horse. He had evidently heard them coming, for he stood by his plough now, his face turned in their direction. As he saw Sholto's red head emerge from the trees, he gave a loud and joyful halloo, and ran towards them surprisingly spryly for his age, which must have been eighty at least. At the shout, David saw another man, a tall thin person, appear in the cottage doorway, stoop to pass under the lintel, and come hurrying to meet them.

The old man went to Juniper's head, pouring questions at Sholto in a dialect David found difficult to understand, and ignoring the other three, but the tall man evidently recognized the King, for he went down on one knee in the mud.

"Your Majesty!" he exclaimed. "Your Majesty, you are welcome to Dragon's End." And he indicated the cottage with a majestic gesture which suggested a castle at least.

"You may rise, friend," replied the King rather testily, "and help me off this animal. He and I are heartily sick of each other."

The cottager's rather long, solemn face was suddenly lighted by a smile which disappeared at once when he perceived that the King was in no smiling mood and had not meant to jest. He went to the horse's head and assisted the King to dismount. His Majesty was plainly so exhausted and stiff that he could hardly stand. Smith and Sholto had also dismounted.

"This is Master Hugh Winter, sir," Sholto told the King. "One of your most loyal subjects. You will be safe in his care."

David, forgetting all discretion, stammered: "H-Hugh Winter, did you say? Hugh Winter?"

"That's my name, young man," answered the cottager. "And are you not going to dismount? You look weary enough."

"I don't think I shall be able to stand up," said David dolefully. "But I was just surprised. You're my uncle. Kate and I came to look for you."

It sounded so ordinary, said just like that, and his new-found uncle did not turn pale or exclaim. He merely looked at David rather quizzically as Sholto lifted him down.

"My nephew David, are you?" he asked. "Well, wonders will never cease! What have you done with your sister Kate?"

"I don't know where she is," David admitted.

"She's safe," Sholto said.

"Then, David, let us take his word for it, shall we? We'll go in and administer liniment, and talk when you have had a rest." Then suddenly he smiled, a merry smile mostly in the eyes, which made his long, plain face look very pleasant. "I'm glad to see you," he said, "so long as you didn't bring Clarence and Marion."

"Oh no!" exclaimed David, horrified at the idea.

He staggered into the cottage behind the King, who had quite obviously given up all hope of looking dignified. Smith and Sholto stayed outside to see to the horses, and Hugh ushered his oddly assorted visitors into a small, low kitchen.

"There's a room at the back where Your Majesty may rest," he said, throwing open a door. "And as for you, David, you'd better have a shake-down in the kitchen. The settle is comfortable enough with cushions and rugs."

The King, signifying with a gesture that he needed no further attendance, disappeared into the inner room and closed the door. Hugh grunted at it.

"I'll have to light a fire, though," he said. "It's cold in that room. There aren't many luxuries here in this bachelor establishment, I fear, but he shall at least have warmth. Lie down, David, if you will."

David lay down on the settle, quite weak from weariness, while his uncle, kindly but rather unhandily, helped him off with his wet clothes then covered him over with rugs. After that, feeling warm and comfortable, he watched Hugh collect sticks from a wood box in the corner for lighting a fire. The little kitchen was very warm, and the heat made him grow drowsier and drowsier, until at last he fell fast asleep, and slept through a good deal of coming and going.

He woke slowly, with the feeling that he must have slept for many hours. He moved cautiously, and found that he was still agonizingly stiff.

"Hullo, are you awake?" asked someone.

"Kate!" David sat up with a jerk, only to lie down again with a stifled exclamation. Kate giggled.

"Sholto said you would have to eat your dinner off the mantelpiece," she said, coming over and perching herself on the edge of his improvised bed.

"It's most uncomfortable," David agreed, "to put it mildly. But I am glad to see you, Kate, and are you really quite all right?" Before she could answer he had started laughing.

"Whatever is the matter?" asked Kate rather indignantly.

"You do look funny in those clothes!"

"I like them," replied Kate defiantly. "And they are much more comfortable than my others."

"I wish Aunt Marion could see you," said David. "She'd have a fit. But seriously—how did you get here, Kate?"

"I'll tell you my adventures," she said, "while you eat something—and then you can tell me yours."

She ladled some porridge into a bowl for him and brought it over. He ate it hungrily, and followed it up with ham and newly baked crusty bread, while she told him how her pony had carried her right into the arms of the Prince of Tomay.

"Then I stayed at the farm," she ended, "with the Princess. I was very worried about you, but they said that it would be all right, and it was. I told them who our uncle was, and they brought me here, and, lo and behold, there you were, fast asleep on the settle."

Then David, who was feeling much refreshed by now, related his adventures.

"You are lucky!" his sister exclaimed when he had finished. "You've helped to rescue the King, and I've hardly done a thing."

"It must be very late." David had scrambled out of the improvized bed, and was now gingerly feeling his legs. "Where's everybody else?"

"Uncle Hugh is outside with Allen and Sholto. Last time I looked out they were all standing round a horse, which apparently is lame or something. The Prince of Tomay left after he brought me here this morning, and I believe he was going to Ree City. The King is still asleep."

"What do you think of Uncle Hugh, Kate?"

"I think he is a great deal nicer than Uncle Clarence," said Kate; and then added with a twinkle in her eye, "It makes me laugh to think how frightened I secretly was at the thought of what he might be like!"

They went outside together and David, at Kate's suggestion, washed rather sketchily at the pump.

"Brr—it is cold!" he exclaimed.

"It's nearly winter," Kate remarked. "But it is funny—I don't mind the cold here nearly so much as I did in the city. I think that when one can get out and move about it is easier to keep warm. Besides, these clothes are most sensible, however funny they may look."

New Plans

THE two children went out into the glade before
the cottage. It was a sunny autumn day and all
the leaves had been washed clean by the recent
storm. The earth was very muddy under foot, and
there was a pleasant after-rain smell which David sniffed
appreciatively.

"I did get tired of Perigal Castle," he said. "You can't
think what a dismal place it is. It has a fusty smell to it
too—mouldy."

"I was terribly afraid they would hurt you," confessed
Kate. "I hope we don't get separated again."

"Hullo, David, and how are you feeling?" It was
Sholto, who had come up behind them with their uncle.

"I can hardly walk," David confessed with a grin.
"But I don't care because it's such a relief to be free
again. I think I ought to thank you, for if it hadn't
been for you I would still be a prisoner."

"And if it hadn't been for you the King would still
be a prisoner. If you hadn't sent Smith to Mistress

Fagan's we would never have managed the escape. It is bouquets all round, so let's dispense with them."

"I haven't had a chance to talk to you two yet," said Hugh Winter. "Do you want to go back to Ree City? I ought to let your Uncle Clarence know that you are safe somehow."

Both children's faces had fallen.

"Oh, don't send us back!" cried Kate piteously. "It was dreadful there."

"Dreadful? How, dreadful?" Uncle Hugh wanted to know. "Come and tell me about it."

He sat down on a bench outside the cottage door and indicated that Kate and David should sit on each side of him.

Kate tried to explain the dreadfulness of life in Milward Street.

"We were only half alive," she said. "We could never go out on our own, and I was never allowed to do things with David, but always had to trail around with Fanny and Mistress Heebes. She was the governess. I don't think Uncle Clarence and Aunt Marion really liked us very much. We—we weren't wanted there." She flushed painfully and floundered. "But perhaps you would rather not—perhaps we would be a nuisance."

David frowned anxiously.

"I think I am old enough to work," he said. "I don't know how to do anything useful, but I could learn. . . ."

Sholto, who stood near them, looked grave, but his blue eyes were twinkling as he watched Hugh's face.

"Hugh won't let you go to work, David," he said. "He has ideas about education."

"Of course you can learn," Hugh said to David. "But I should be very glad to have you both here if you are willing to stay so much in the wilds. Why, I should like the company."

"Oh, may we really stay?" cried Kate, relief flooding her heart, as she leapt delightedly to her feet. "Oh, good! I love the forest so much—and—and everything!" she embraced her surroundings with a broad gesture. "Oh, thank you, Uncle Hugh! We will be good! I'll cook for you and keep house, and mend your clothes, really I will!" And impulsively she flung her arms around her uncle's neck and kissed him.

Hugh looked pleased, if a little embarrassed.

"Are you sure it is all right?" David asked cautiously. "You see, after being with Uncle Clarence we wouldn't like to be somewhere else where we aren't wanted."

"Of course I am sure," Hugh said firmly. "I'm going to like you both very much, I can see that, and, anyway, we must stick together. After all, blood is thicker than water—I don't count your Uncle Clarence as a relation; he has vinegar running in his veins. I remember him well."

The King came out of the cottage then, and they were all suddenly quiet. He looked at them with sombre eyes, and Hugh hurried to greet him.

"I trust Your Majesty is rested," he said.

"Very well, I thank you," King Roderick replied. He looked about him at the tall beech trees, their few remaining tinted leaves burnished by the sun, but it seemed as if their beauty only hurt him.

"I'll get you some breakfast, sir," Hugh said, and disappeared into the cottage. Kate, who was too happy to be quelled for long, laughed.

"Is it very late, then?" The King looked in a dazzled way at the high sun, and then brought his eyes back to Kate. "You are the girl that took such care of my son," he said.

"I was glad to do it, sir," Kate answered quickly, with a curtsey.

"Do you know where he is now?" asked the King.

"He was with Jane Rider," answered Kate. "But the Princess of Tomay went to fetch him. She said she would bring him here, and then we would all go to the citadel."

"It is good of her," said the King. "And His Highness? Where is he?"

"He has gone to Ree City," answered Sholto. "He wished to see how matters stood there."

"Alone?" the King looked a little alarmed. "Mountmaris would go to any lengths to destroy him."

"He will be safe enough," answered Sholto. "And, after all, Mountmaris's power has no real foundation. He is a brass figure with feet of clay."

"Why so? He seemed all powerful to me," the King said sadly.

Sholto replied: "Because all the power he has is borrowed from Your Majesty. When you cease to back him he will fall. You will see. He has forced himself on a people who do not want him, and he has tried to make himself popular with pageantry and show, but there are plenty who see through that. He is heartily hated by the many he has oppressed."

"And Tomay is well loved," added Roderick quietly.

"He has oppressed no one, and liberated us all," Hugh, who had joined them, put in.

"The King is neither hated nor loved," Roderick said slowly.

There was a constrained silence, and Sholto made an impatient movement.

"Sir——" he was beginning, when they heard hoof-beats coming along the track. A stocky forest pony appeared through the trees, walking steadily. His rider, a woman dressed like a peasant, held a child in front of her.

"Joanna, have you ridden all the way from Fleet like that?" asked Sholto as he went to the pony's head.

Joanna of Tomay smiled as she slid to the ground.

"It seemed the best way to pass unnoticed," she said. "There are plenty of the White Guard about, and I knew that if they stopped my carriage there'd be a riot among our people, so I decided not to risk it."

She came across to the King, who had not moved, and curtseyed. The child leaned against her shoulder and gazed gravely at his father.

"Princess . . ." began Roderick, but seemed unable to say more. He looked at his son as though he could not tear his eyes away.

But Louis had seen Kate and started to laugh.

"Oh, he remembers me!" cried Kate, and rushed to hug him without ceremony. "Hullo, baby! Was Jane Rider good to you, then?"

"Come into the cottage," suggested Joanna. "May we, Hugh? Let us see how he can stand. Jane says he can stand quite well now."

Inside, Hugh had set a meal. King Roderick was still very quiet and restrained, but Joanna appeared quite unembarrassed by his presence. She put Louis down on the floor, and he soon pulled himself up by the table-leg and staggered across to Kate, who was highly delighted at such favouritism. She and David squatted on the floor and played with him, while their elders planned an exodus to the safety of the citadel.

The King was evidently very much troubled about the Prince of Tomay's safety, but both Hugh and Sholto seemed confident that he was well able to take care of himself. Joanna looked a little worried, Kate thought, but she did not express any fears. She only said quietly:

"My husband thought it best to go himself, sire. He asked me to beg you to allow us to escort Your Majesty and the Prince to the citadel, where you will be safe for the time being."

"You are very kind, Your Highness," the King answered gravely, "and I thank you for your care for our safety. But there is work to be done; I cannot be idle while my kingdom is at the mercy of this traitor."

They looked at him in silence, a little surprised at this unexpected desire for action, and Sholto was about to speak when he was interrupted by the urgent beat of galloping hoofs approaching the glade.

"Wait, sir." Sholto was up and outside in a moment, closely followed by Hugh. David would have gone too, but Joanna restrained him.

"Stay quiet," she advised. "You are an escaped prisoner, David, remember that."

But the rider was evidently a friend. They heard him cry out as he pulled up his blowing pony:

"News! Mountmaris has burnt the village at All Saints Dale. He says Tomay has seized the person of the King and for that he will punish all the foresters. He hanged three men at All Saints because they resisted him."

"It's Mr. Verey!" cried Kate, who had recognized the voice. She ran out and the others followed her. Mr. Verey bowed low to the King and to Joanna and told them his news again, less breathlessly now.

"The men of the forest are gathering at Fleet," he ended grimly. "They will not stand for this!"

"But what will they do?" Joanna asked, white-faced, forgetting the King's presence in her anxiety.

"Drive the traitor out of the forest—what else? The Prince will lead us," Verey said.

"No," protested Joanna quickly. "That would be civil war, and Adrian would never want that. He has gone to Ree City because he believes that the basis of Mount-maris's power can be destroyed there and the traitor cast out without bloodshed."

"Bloodshed!" echoed Sholto sharply. "He deserves all he gets."

"But his men follow him because they believe him loyal, Sholto," she pleaded. "They are not knowingly traitors, and they would suffer as well as he; and civil wars cause so much bitterness and misery. How well I know that! The scars in Mir are not yet healed. . . ."

"Nor ours from the invasion," the King added. "No, we cannot have Prosperitans fighting each other."

"I suppose it could lead to that," Sholto admitted reasonably. "But how are we to stop them? Who but Tomay can hold the forest men once they are roused?"

"I think I could for a while," Joanna said. "After all I am their Princess, although I am a foreigner, and they respect me for Adrian's sake. And he will not stay away long. He will hear what has happened, and come back to take care of his own people."

The King smiled a little.

"You have great faith in the Prince, madame," he said.

"I have learned to believe in him," she answered simply.

"But, Joanna," Sholto protested, "while you hold your men back, what is to prevent Mountmaris from doing further damage? He might pillage half the villages in the forest if we do not make a move to stop him."

He turned to Verey quickly: "Could we persuade the people on the border to move into the forest?"

Verey shook his head.

"They had to do that for the Uralians," he said. "And

their homes have been sacked all too recently. You won
get them to leave now, and you can't command them.
They are a free people, and must be led, not driven. The
Prince is their only authority, and he knows how to deal
with them."

Sholto frowned and ruffled his fiery head in an effort
to think of some way out of the dilemma. The King, who
had been listening quietly, now said: "I think it best that
the Princess of Tomay should go to Fleet as she suggests,
and hold the foresters back for as long as she can. But
I do not think that we need to evacuate the villages on
the border. I will go and meet Mountmaris's army. I do
not believe the men are disloyal themselves. They may
not have realized that I was a prisoner."

"What? Go yourself?" exclaimed Hugh. "That would
be far too dangerous, sire."

"It is a brave plan," Sholto said, looking at the King
with new respect. "But it is too great a risk for Your
Majesty to take. We do not know that they will be loyal."

"Couldn't we ask Smith?" David suggested timidly,
and then blushed at having spoken before his elders.

His Uncle Clarence would have put him in his place,
but his Uncle Hugh said: "A good thought, David!"

And Sholto added: "Smith is round in the stable with
Allen. I'll go now and speak with him," and went
forthwith.

Joanna was looking a little troubled.

"Sire," she said, "you may be putting yourself into the
enemy's hands again, and the next time it will not be so
easy to rescue you."

"But you will have my son, the Prince, safe, madame,"
answered the King gravely. "And Tomay would uphold

him and the kingdom, I know, if anything
pen to me."

rse he would," Joanna said. "But, oh, how I
ere here now! I do not like this venture. It is
too da g rous for you."

"I do not feel that I would be much loss to the
country," said Roderick bitterly. "I have done it little
good so far."

"Sire," protested Joanna gently, "you must not
say that." Sholto returned before she could say any
more.

"Smith is certain that nearly all the Protector's soldiers
are ignorant of the real position," he said. "But, even so,
it is a great risk. Will you still do it, sire?"

"It is the only course open to me," said Roderick
simply. "I will go alone."

"No." Sholto shook his head stubbornly. "Not
alone." Then, as the King glared at him, he smiled
suddenly and bent his knee. "Your Majesty," he said,
"in return for my services yesterday for which you were
good enough to express gratitude, I beg the privilege of
accompanying you on this adventure."

"Damned cheek, but nicely put," murmured Hugh.

"You are mocking," protested the King, half angry.

"No," said Sholto, his smile vanishing. "I was never
more serious in my life." And he added quietly, "I would
like a share in Your Majesty's honour."

Roderick flushed, as he answered, not very steadily:
"Very well—you shall go with me if you wish."

"You will need a guide, sire," said Joanna quickly,
"and Sholto knows the forest well."

The King nodded.

"Then perhaps Master Winter would take my son to Tomay, Princess," he said, "since you go to Fleet."

"I will look after him," offered Kate.

"That's right, Kate," agreed Hugh. "You and David and I will go."

But David, throwing caution to the winds, cried:

"Couldn't I go with you and Sholto, sire? I could be useful as a page, perhaps."

"Are you prepared to risk falling into the Protector's hands again, boy?" asked the King.

David changed colour, but he said stoutly:

"If we go together I am not afraid, and it is not right for a king to be so poorly attended."

"Will your blisters let you ride, David?" teased Sholto.

Although Sholto and Joanna and Hugh were all against it— or perhaps because they were—the King gave David his way, and everyone set about preparing for departure.

XVI

The Troubles of Kate

KATE and David had a quarrel about the latter's determination to accompany the King, and because they had never quarrelled much, having always been in offensive alliance against their aunt and uncle, the event was earth-shaking.

Kate wept, and said that she did not see why they should be separated again. She begged to be allowed to accompany her brother, but all the grown-ups were against this, as well as David himself.

"It isn't fair!" she stormed, when they were alone together. "Why should you have an adventure that I can't share? If I can't come as well, I don't think you ought to go."

"Don't be silly, Kate," David reproved her, with maddening superiority. "Girls can't do everything that boys do."

"They can! They can!" cried Kate furiously. "Where is the Princess? I'll ask her."

But Joanna had departed already for Fleet, and there

was no one of Kate's sex to uphold her. She felt desperate.

"I am coming with you," she said.

"You can't," answered David. "His Majesty would forbid it."

"I am coming, I am coming!" she cried excitedly.

David glared at her in despair.

"Do be sensible, Kate," he begged, in a last effort to pacify her. "You know you can't, really."

"Oh, you are insufferable! I hate you!" sobbed his sister, well aware that she was helpless.

David turned on his heel without a word and left her. He could not help feeling sorry for her, though he thought she was behaving very stupidly, and he looked very dejected when he joined Sholto and Hugh, who were saddling up.

Sholto looked at him and said quietly:

"If you've changed your mind, David, and would rather go with Hugh, no one will think any the worse of you."

David shook his head.

"I want to come," he said.

"You would be wiser not to," advised Hugh, who looked troubled. "His Majesty would understand."

"No, it isn't that I am worried about," David said, and then he added honestly, "Although I am a bit scared, of course—but I wouldn't change now for anything. No, it's Kate. She's in a great rage because I'm going without her." He hung his head as he went on, "I know I ought to have thought of her more, because it isn't nice for her to have to stay behind, but I can't always stay where she wants me to be, can I?" He looked pleadingly at Hugh and Sholto to see if they understood.

"Poor Kate," Hugh said, "it is hard for her—but I think you are quite right. She has got to realize that you can't always do everything together. She'll get over it."

David looked doubtful.

"She's very miserable," he said unhappily. "And she is being most unreasonable. I'm afraid she may do something silly."

But Kate was back with them before they set out. She had heard the baby crowing in the cottage, and gone in to play with him. She came out now with him in her arms, and although her eyes were red and swollen she was resigned and calm again.

"That's right, Kate," said Hugh. "I don't know what I should do without you. I must confess I'm no nurse-maid."

Kate looked at him rather resentfully, and hugged Louis, who laughed, quite unaffected by the tense atmosphere. The King had come out of the cottage, and Sholto held his stirrup while he mounted. David settled rather painfully in his saddle, but was determined not to show his discomfort.

"Goodbye, Kate," he said.

"Goodbye," she answered, with a forlorn sniff.

"Don't worry too much, Kate," Sholto said cheerfully. "We'll take care of him all right."

Kate managed to smile, but she was worried. The King looked white and anxious, and she knew that Sholto and Hugh both thought the expedition dangerous because they had tried to dissuade David from going.

She stood in a daze watching them ride away between the trees until she felt a hand on her shoulder.

"Come, Kate," said Hugh. "Now we must prepare for our own journey."

She had no time to brood because he kept her busy hurrying to and fro from that moment until he and she were perched in the wagon which rocked and lurched wildly as the sturdy little cob drew it along the uneven track.

Hugh began to talk to her about the forest.

"You'll have to know all about it if it's to be your home," he said. "Do you think you will like living in the forest, Kate?"

"Oh yes!" she cried, her misery momentarily forgotten. "I never was in such a beautiful place. I love the trees—but I tell you what I love best: the open spaces on the high ground, and the strips of moorland. We came across one on the way here from Master Verey's farm, and he said there was a great stretch of it to the west."

"Witchwold," Hugh said. "It's wild country. A great many people are afraid of it. The story goes that a terrible monster lived there once, in the bottom of Fardy mere, and ravaged the country far and wide, carrying victims away to his lair. Some of the peasants believe his descendants live there still, but the story says he was killed by a hero, and there is no record of any descendants."

"Do you know a lot of stories, Uncle Hugh?" asked Kate.

He laughed, and answered: "A fair number. I was a schoolmaster, you know, before His Highness gave me Dragon's End, and schoolmasters have to tell stories.

Sometimes it is the only way that they can keep their unruly pupils quiet."

"I've always hated lessons," confessed Kate. "But David likes them and is good at them. His tutor was quite nice, and taught him all kinds of interesting things. I don't think I should have minded learning from him, but Mistress Heebes, the governess, was horrid."

"Well, let us hope you will like learning from me," said Hugh, "for I shall have to teach you both for a time if you come to live at Dragon's End. The nearest schools are too far away until you know the country a bit and are safe on ponies."

"David is getting quite good at riding," Kate said. And then, remembering the errand on which her brother had gone, she added, her face puckered with anxiety: "I do hope he will be all right."

"Don't you worry," Hugh said—but Kate suspected him of sounding more confident than he felt—"Sholto's luck is good, and he'll take care of David."

"You none of you seem to have much faith in the poor King," remarked Kate thoughtfully.

Hugh answered with a sigh: "He hasn't given us any cause hitherto. But this is a brave thing he is doing now —unless—but he can't side with Mountmaris. I'm certain of that."

He gathered up the reins and clicked his tongue, and the cob broke into a trot. They had come out onto a broader track—an apology for a road.

"This is the stretch of our route that I like least," Hugh said. "There's a possibility Mountmaris's patrols may have reached this track. They're likely to stop any attempt on our part to get the King and the Prince to the citadel. I think it might be advisable for you to keep under cover, Kate, with the baby."

Kate obediently scrambled back into the rear of the wagon, and crouched down there, holding Louis in her arms. The sun was shining down on the broad track between the trees, and she was sheltered from the wind and reasonably warm. She had become quite used by now to her forest clothes, and wondered how she had ever been able to bear the uncomfortable garments that Aunt Marion had believed suitable for a growing girl.

She sat with her back propped against the side of the wagon, relaxed and half asleep, while the child sat upright in her lap, catching at the shadows of the leaves as they flickered by, until in time he fell asleep, lulled by the motion.

The rocking did not make Kate feel sick if she relaxed to it, she discovered, and, in spite of her anxiety about David, a sense of physical well-being made her almost contented.

"You can come back to the front soon," Hugh called. "We're nearly through the——" His voice faded suddenly, and Kate, sitting up in alarm, could tell by his back that he was wary and alert. But he did not pull up the horse.

"Kate," he said, "there are men hidden at the side of the track ahead. They may be the Protector's men. Will you do what I tell you at once?"

"Yes, Uncle Hugh," answered Kate, trembling.

"I shall slow down in a moment as the track narrows. When I say 'now' slip over the tailboard with the child and go and hide in the bushes. Stay there till I return to fetch you. Can you do that, Kate?"

"Yes."

"God guard you! Now!"

Kate, holding the child carefully, let herself down over the tailboard. She landed on her feet and fled into the bushes while the wagon still screened her. In the hazel thicket she spread her shawl and laid the child carefully upon it, and then crouched as close to the track as she dared, peering between the branches. Through the rumbling and creaking of the wagon she heard shouts, and then she saw about a dozen men come out of the trees and run towards it. She heard the crack of Hugh's whip, and the clumsy equipage rattled away at a great pace, with the soldiers running after it, shouting and yelling. Further on up the ride—by craning her neck she could just see—Hugh pulled up, and she saw the soldiers jump into the wagon to search it. She gasped, thinking what a narrow escape the Prince had had. After a while the wagon went on again, and this time the soldiers walked beside it, escorting it.

"Oh dear," thought poor Kate, "however is he to come back and fetch me now? And what will they do to him?"

There was nothing for it but to settle down and wait as she had been told to do, and she supposed her uncle would eventually shake off the soldiers. After all, they could have nothing against him. So Kate sat down beside the baby and waited.

It was very still in the forest, so still that every time a bird or some little animal rustled in the bushes Kate nearly jumped out of her skin. She grew cold and soon found that her teeth were chattering, while the baby woke and started to wail. He, too, was cold, and hungry and miserable. Kate was terrified that his crying would bring somebody, but nobody came, and she could not pacify him. She herself was near to tears. She walked up and down in a tiny clearing with the baby to try and warm them both, and as it grew dark Kate began to wish that somebody *would* come—anybody. It was very frightening to be alone in the forest at night.

Louis slept at last, huddled, heavy and exhausted, against her shoulder, and Kate found that it was she who was crying now, the tears chasing each other down her cheeks. It had become quite dark, and still Uncle Hugh didn't come.

Suddenly Kate stopped her sobbing. She could hear horses' hoofs approaching and men talking.

"I tell you he must have seen you," one of the men was saying, "and hidden whatever he had. Then he led you off, and like fools you fell into his trap."

"We'd no reason to suspect him," said another voice gloomily. They were almost level now. Kate crouched down, trembling, but unfortunately as she did so the low branch of a holly bush brushed against the baby's cheek. He awoke with a loud wail.

"My God! What's that?" cried one of the men in terror-struck tones. "This forest at night . . ."

"Come on, you fool!" shouted the other. "That was what we were looking for."

Kate fled blindly, stumbling in the black darkness. She held the baby with his face against her shoulder to muffle his cries and protect him from the thorns. The branches whipped her cheeks and brambles tore at her skirt. Then she fell over a root, twisted as she fell to save the child, and landed with a fierce jar on her wrist. She was conscious of a sickening, shooting pain up her arm, then heard her pursuers crashing through the brush, while the baby's shrieks were redoubled. Noise and pain seemed to whirl round her all joined in one frantic maelstrom, and then she fainted.

XVII

A Bloodless Victory

D AVID was thankful to think that at any rate Kate would be safe.

"She must be in the Citadel by this time," he thought, when they had ridden a long way. "Hugh said it wasn't far."

He and Sholto rode one on each side of the King when the tracks were broad enough, and when they had to go in single file Sholto led and David brought up the rear, his pony jogging to keep up with their bigger horses.

The journey was uneventful until they reached Kerislade, where they fell in with an advance party of the Protector's men. These were a dismounted detachment of the White Guard, and they had strung themselves out across the village street to challenge all comers. The officer in charge called on the King and his two companions to halt.

"Stand where you are!" he ordered. "State your names and business."

The King did not rein in his horse, but let him walk quietly on. Sholto, who had been a little behind him, drew level, and as the soldiers ran up, and one of them attempted to seize the bridle of the King's horse, he hastily retreated, finding the point of Sholto's sword unpleasantly near his throat.

"Will you resist the Protector's orders?" shouted the enraged officer.

"You are speaking to your King!" cried Sholto.

"The King!" The officer started forward, and one of his men echoed: "The King! It is the King."

Miraculously the assailants who had been crowding upon them fell back, and many of them went down on one knee in the road.

"Sire," gasped the officer, "forgive me, I did not know. . . . They said that you were ill. . . ."

Roderick sat silent for a moment, bare-headed, his face stern and pale. Then he said:

"Will you conduct me to the Lord Protector, lieutenant?"

"Sire"—the lieutenant seemed alarmed—"the Lord Protector's orders . . ."

"I am the King, lieutenant," Roderick said coldly.

"Yes, sire," the lieutenant said. Then he tried again, indicating Sholto: "This man—we have orders to arrest him as a traitor to Your Majesty."

"*He* is no traitor," answered the King, with heavy emphasis.

"Sire"—the lieutenant bowed his head—"I am at your Majesty's service."

"Then you will escort me to the Lord Protector at once, lieutenant."

"Yes, sire." The lieutenant saluted smartly. Then he turned and gave an order to his troop. In a few minutes they were all horsed, and the King and his two companions were clattering merrily along the road escorted by a score of soldiers. David felt rather grand, but Roderick looked grim, and Sholto was plainly not at his ease.

It was not far from Kerislade to the Lord Protector's camp on the edge of the forest. They came over the crest of the hill, and the sight before them drew an exclamation from Sholto.

"He has a veritable army!"

"His lordship has to deal with rebels in Tomay," answered the lieutenant, who had drawn level.

"The army was for that, was it?" Sholto asked. "To burn houses and hang peaceable people at All Saints."

"The Protector deals justice," answered the lieutenant indignantly. Sholto opened his mouth to retort, but a glance from the King silenced him. At the sight of his glum face, David could not help wanting to laugh.

"With your permission, Your Majesty," said the lieutenant, "I will ride ahead and inform the Lord Protector of your arrival."

The King gave his consent to this, and the lieutenant, followed by two of his men, cantered away down the hill, while the rest of them followed more slowly. They were near the edge of the camp when the Lord Protector himself, with a magnificent detachment of his White Guard, rode out to meet them. If he felt any perturbation at this unexpected turn of events, he did not show it. He leapt from his horse, and bent to kiss the King's hand.

"Your Majesty!" he exclaimed. "I rejoice to see you safe and sound. I feared that you had fallen into the hands of your enemies."

"I fell into good hands, your grace," answered the King quietly.

But the Protector cried: "I am afraid Your Majesty has been deceived. You have a traitor with you now. . . ."

The King silenced him with a gesture.

"My two attendants are my loyal subjects," he said. And then he went on, "Why have you raised this magnificent army, my lord?"

"To subdue Your Majesty's enemies," answered the Duke at once, with a baleful glance at Sholto and David.

"Parade your men, my lord duke," ordered the King. "I would like to see what array you have collected on my behalf."

Mountmaris remounted. He looked flustered now, and, wheeling his horse, he snapped a command at one of his officers.

"Shoot down those two traitors!" he cried. "But spare the King!"

"The devil!" exclaimed Sholto. "Stand away, David! They might hit the King, and it's his life Mountmaris wants, the dirty trickster!"

He made Juniper sidle away as he spoke. Some of the soldiers had levelled their muskets, but no one fired, for the King had raised his hand.

"I forbid it!" he cried. "St. George—and you, boy— stand close. They shall not shoot my servants!"

A high-ranking officer laid his hand on Mountmaris's rein.

"My lord," he protested, "what are you about? The King might well be hurt, even killed."

"My zeal makes me thoughtless," said the Protector, white to the lips now. "This way, sire."

There was a great blowing of bugles, and the men hurried to parade before their king. Roderick, still closely attended by Sholto and David, rode up to a little knoll in the centre of the camp. They had no sooner taken up their station there, with the discomfited Protector and his officers beside them, when a messenger rode up with news for Mountmaris. Judging by his condition and that of his horse, he had ridden hard and far, and his face was so drawn and haggard that David hardly recognized his old enemy Captain Varek.

"My lord!" cried the captain, before the Protector could forestall him. "Tomay is in Ree City and has stirred the Great Council against you! He has had Forester released and declared your grace a traitor."

His voice faded away as he saw the King, and realized that he had given his master away.

"Your Majesty!" he said, and fell on his knees in the mud.

The King regarded him coldly, then turned to the horrified-looking general who stood near them.

"General Hart," he ordered, "arrest this man who has had the insolence to call himself Protector of my kingdom."

There was a moment's pause and then the colonel obeyed, and the Protector handed him his sword. Varek knelt still on the trampled grass at the King's feet, his face grey with fear.

"Pardon, Your Majesty," he begged.

The King looked at him with contempt. "Arrest this rat also, general," he said.

The prisoners were taken away, and the general, very much flustered, began trying to explain away his connection with Mountmaris.

"Not now, general," said the King. "You may send to His Highness the Prince of Tomay and ask him if he will attend me as soon as he is able."

"Of course, sire. If Your Majesty wishes to rest there are quarters in a farmhouse at your disposal."

Indeed, Roderick was drooping in his saddle from weariness. Sholto had slid off Juniper and walked at the King's stirrup, for he looked as though he might faint. The red mare followed them by herself, picking her way daintily, and flirting her head. Sholto looked up at the King with pride and affection, and Roderick smiled.

"Have I earned your respect at last, Sholto St. George?" he asked, his words slurred with fatigue.

"You have indeed, sire," said Sholto; adding with a grin. "If the respect of a gipsy is worth anything to you."

"It is worth a great deal," answered the King gravely; and added with a sigh, "so would Tomay's be."

"I am sure you have that, sire," said Sholto.

"Are you?" asked the King. "Well, you know him best."

They reached the farmhouse and the King retired to rest. David could hardly walk without holding on to things.

"Blisters troublesome?" queried Sholto, as he rubbed down Juniper. "Go in, and find yourself some supper."

"I'd rather stay and help," David said. "Sholto. . ."

"Yes?"

"When you said 'stand away' and they were going to shoot did you feel afraid?"

Sholto grinned at him over Juniper's rump.

"State secrets! I would have if there had been time."

David smiled back.

"There wasn't time, was there? But it is a nice surprise to find that one isn't quite such a coward as one feared. I *am* relieved! But I couldn't make my pony go sideways. I had to turn him right round."

Suddenly they were both laughing.

"You'll do," Sholto said approvingly, and when they had sobered down he said: "It was a great stroke of His Majesty's."

The Return of Kate

KATE came round to the consciousness of agonizing pain in her arm which came and went with the movement of a horse. She realized slowly that she was being held in front of a trooper who was riding at a brisk trot. She felt a sensation of panic at her helplessness, and then she remembered the baby. She had not got him. She struggled weakly.

"Keep still, you little fool!" barked the trooper who held her.

"The baby!" gasped Kate.

"He's safe enough," replied the trooper. "But you won't be seeing much more of him; the Lord Protector will see to that. For a couple of children you and your brother have given a lot of trouble."

Kate said desperately:

"But the Lord Protector will kill him, and he's the Prince. You don't understand. You must let me take him."

"Do you think I am going to believe the stories you

choose to make up?" laughed her captor scornfully. "You little trouble-maker!"

"Leave the little girl alone, Royland," the other trooper protested. "She's been through a good deal, and maybe she meant all for the best. The baby is all right, Missie. I have him here with me."

His gruff kindliness heartened Kate a little, but by and by the pain in her arm became so great that she could hardly think clearly. She felt sick with it, but she would not let herself cry, and gritted her teeth to bear it. When they arrived at an inn she hardly knew what was happening to her. She felt herself lifted down, and someone poured something down her throat. She coughed and spluttered.

"Brandy," she said, recognizing it, "I don't like it," and she turned her head away.

Royland laughed, and a shrill, female voice called him a brute—

"You hold your tongue!" the trooper shouted. "See to that child—that's what I'm paying you for—and leave the girl alone. She's my prisoner."

Kate sat on a stool near the fire in the bar, with her back propped against the wall. The woman brought her some food, but she could not eat. The troopers were talking with the innkeeper and his man at the bar. Their loud voices buzzed in Kate's head, and she did not really grasp the meaning of what they were saying.

"The news is that the Protector's finished," the innkeeper was stoutly maintaining. "Tomay has cut the ground from under his feet at the capital. No one knows what he will do now."

"Good riddance to bad rubbish!" exclaimed the shrill-voiced woman boldly. "We've had enough of troopers getting us out of bed at nights!"

"That's treason, ma'am, and I'll remember it," Royland said.

"And the men of the forest are gathered at Fleet," went on the landlord. "They'll avenge those who died at All Saints."

Royland rose, looking at him scornfully.

"I've no leisure to listen to idle talk," he said. "It's time we were getting on. Come you, Morris."

His companion rose reluctantly, and the landlady brought Louis. She had tucked him into a small laundry-basket, and Morris had to balance this across the withers of his tired horse, while Royland took Kate again, lifting her with little ceremony. His roughness hurt her but she would not cry out.

"Be more careful with the lass," Morris was moved to say. "She's hurt her wrist."

"I'm careful enough," his companion replied shortly.

They travelled on, and Kate gathered from their talk that they were heading for the Protector's camp, and once she and the baby were in his hands she felt that they could not hope to escape. She would most certainly be separated from the Prince and no one would know what had become of him. She must make an effort now, and think of something.

"Heroes in stories never let a hurt arm hinder them," she told herself firmly, "nor long odds." And she sat up in front of Royland and began to look about her.

It was just beginning to get light, and they were crossing a stretch of moorland. There was a ground mist, and the air was moist and chill. Even as she looked ahead Morris looked back and said:

"There's a horseman coming!"

They saw him for a moment against the sky behind, and then he came down the dip towards them, a moving shadow in the dimness, with pale mist swirling round his horse's legs. When he saw them he slowed to a walk.

Royland pinned Kate to him with his bridle arm, and with his right hand loosened a pistol in its holster.

"He'll not molest us," he told Morris, "but it's as well to be on our guard in this accursed country."

The approaching rider hailed them.

"It's a cold morning to be abroad in!" he called cheerily.

And Kate recognized the voice, and instantly she knew that Royland had also, for his whole body stiffened. She screamed out: "Take care!" and twisted herself wildly, kicking at Royland's horse even as the explosion of his pistol crashed close to her ear. The horse reared, and the next thing Kate knew she was rolling on the ground practically under its feet.

"It's Tomay!" she heard Royland shout to Morris. "Fire, you fool, fire!" Then he was swearing at his horse. The feet of another horse flashed past Kate, and two more shots rang out simultaneously. Then she heard wildly galloping hoofs thudding away down the track.

"Oh!" sobbed Kate, putting her hand in front of her eyes.

"Kate, Kate, don't cry." It was Tomay who lifted her up and carried her to the side of the track.

"Then you're not dead?" she queried shakily, looking up at him.

"No, thanks to you. Why, child, what have you done to your wrist?"

But Kate did not answer.

"The baby!" she cried in a panic.

"He's still here, missie," said another voice, and she saw that Morris still sat his horse in the track, laundry-basket and all. The baby was sitting up and now started to wail.

"And why didn't you fire when your friend asked you to?" Adrian asked Morris.

"Well, sir, it's like this," Morris said: "if it wasn't for you we should still be under the Uralians as like as not. Even for the Lord Protector I wouldn't lift a hand against you, sir. Royland can go back and report if he pleases."

"He won't find his old master to report to," said Adrian quietly; "the king is in command at All Saints."

"Oh," said Kate, "then David is all right?"

"Quite all right. Now, Kate, if our friend here would lend us his grand regimental scarf, we'll try to make your arm more comfortable."

He fixed the swollen arm gently in a sling made from Morris's silk scarf. The latter entertained the baby by singing nursery rhymes very much out of tune, so that Kate found herself laughing weakly. Tomay then wrapped her in his cloak and lifted her on to his horse.

"Now we must go," he said, "but we'll go slowly."

They walked their horses into the camp at All Saints about twenty minutes later, a bedraggled and weary party, and were directed at once to the farmhouse where the King had his headquarters. A surprised-looking sentry informed them that the Princess of Tomay was there, also Mr. Winter and David. Hugh met them at the door. He looked very tired, and when he saw Kate his face crumpled with relief.

"Kate!" he said. "Kate! We've been scouring the country for you, ever since the King had me released. And the Prince?"

"He's here," Adrian said. "Hugh, can you find a surgeon? The child's broken her wrist. Where's Sholto?"

"Out searching still," said Hugh. "His Majesty retired, and Her Highness and David on our orders, but I doubt if they have slept."

He hurried off in search of a surgeon, and soon Kate found herself surrounded by people, and being kissed and congratulated. David kept on saying: "Kate, I thought you were lost—and, after all, you had the most adventures." The King looked quite human when he smiled and told her she was a brave girl and thanked her for being so faithful to the little Prince.

"And now Kate ought to be left in peace," Joanna said. "She looks quite dazed still—and here's the surgeon."

Kate forgot she was a heroine then and began to tremble.

"Will it—will it hurt much?" she asked.

"It will soon be over, little lady," answered the surgeon cheerfully. "We'll send all your friends away, shall we?"

Kate looked despairingly at Tomay.

"I'm not very brave," she faltered. "Will you please stay with me, sir?"

"Of course I will," he answered.

"Oh, poor Kate!" whispered David as he went out. "Is she very badly hurt?"

"No, it's not serious, and it will soon get better," Joanna reassured him, "once it's set. Don't worry, David. Lots of people break arms, you know. Come and help me feed your baby."

"Our baby!" David smiled. "He feels almost like that."

"Poor mite! It's a wonder he's survived so well," said Joanna, as Louis sat up in her lap drinking warm milk. She had washed him and made him comfortable, and after he had drunk some of the milk he curled up in the laundry-basket and went to sleep.

"He seems to know when he's among friends," said Hugh.

"Babies always know," declared Joanna.

Later Adrian came out to them and said that Kate's arm was set, and the doctor had given her something to make her sleep.

"It was a clean break, my lady," said the surgeon, who had followed him out. "And I don't think any harm will result from the delay in setting it. Good night, my lady."

"Good night," said Joanna, "and thank you. Adrian, if you will carry Kate upstairs I'll undress her and put her to bed. David, you go and get some sleep."

"Come, David," said Hugh. "You're half asleep on your feet already."

"It seems funny to be going to bed in the morning," David remarked drowsily; but he obeyed.

XIX

Conclusion

MORRIS and Smith, who had appointed themselves maids of all work, were cooking a meal
and arguing in the farm kitchen about the best
way to make omelette, when a soldier came and said that
a lady and a gentleman who had travelled from Ree City
by coach were declaring that they had come to fetch
David and Katharine Holt.

"Tell them they are asleep and can't come," said Smith.

"What about some breakfast?" It was Sholto who had
just arrived back from his search to find his quarry
safely returned, much to his relief.

"Ready in a minute, sir," said Smith. "There's a
gentleman and a lady asking for Master David and Miss
Kate."

"More people after David and Kate?" queried Sholto,
amused. "They must be the most hunted children in
Prosperito. I'll go and see who it is."

He went out, and there, standing in the churned-up
mud of the yard and holding a pomander to her nose,

stood an indignant-looking lady, attended by an even more indignant-looking gentleman, who was trying to persuade the sentry to let him into the house.

"I tell you I have a pass!" he was shouting, waving a sheaf of papers.

"That pass won't do now, that won't," answered the sentry firmly. "It is signed by Captain Varek and admits

you to an audience with the Protector. That ain't no good now. They're both in prison."

The gentleman went red and then white and drew back in alarm, whereupon Sholto, who had been enjoying the situation, felt called upon to intervene.

"Can I help you, perhaps?" he asked politely, bowing to the lady.

The couple looked at him disgustedly. He was dressed in a most ungentlemanly fashion, and was still travel-worn and mud-splashed from his all-night search. Weariness gave him a slightly dissipated appearance.

"Fellow," announced the gentleman haughtily, "I have a pass admitting me to an audience with the Lord Protector."

"The Duke of Craglands is the prisoner of his Majesty the King," answered Sholto.

"That makes things a little awkward," said the gentleman. "I must see someone in authority at once. I have come to fetch my niece and nephew, who ran away, and whom his lord—the Protector detained for me."

Seeing that Mountmaris was now a prisoner, Mr. Clarence Holt was plainly not going to accord him the courtesy of a title.

"Oh dear!" burst out the lady. "Those poor children! Whatever can have happened to them? And after I brought them up with my own little daughter and made such sacrifices for them."

"Ungrateful little things," her husband said. "Running away like that!"

"I find it intriguing that the Protector took such interest in helping you to find these children," Sholto could not resist saying.

"My name is Holt," said the gentleman haughtily, ignoring this impudent curiosity. "Clarence Holt. And I should be grateful if you would inform someone in authority that I have come."

"If you will come into the house," Sholto suggested, "perhaps we can find you some breakfast."

"Breakfast!" echoed Mistress Holt faintly. "At this hour!"

"Well, every one was up very late last night," Sholto explained. "I haven't been to bed myself yet, but I think I'll have some breakfast first."

He led them past the sentry, who saluted him, greatly to their surprise, and through the kitchen and into the farm front parlour, where Smith had lighted a fire.

"Breakfast in a minute, sir," Smith told Sholto.

"But I don't want any breakfast!" Master Holt almost screamed in his exasperation.

And his wife wailed: "We came to fetch our nephew and niece, David and Katharine."

"You will have to talk to Hugh about them," Sholto explained. "Hugh Winter—he is also their uncle."

"Hugh Winter!" exclaimed Master Holt with great scorn. "Has he noticed the children's existence at last?" As he spoke the door opened and David came in. He stopped short in dismay when he saw who was there, and Mistress Holt exclaimed in horror. This shock-headed young ruffian, burnt brown by the sun and wind, and dressed in a ragged shirt and breeches, looked very different from the David who had lived at her house in Ree City.

"David!" she cried in horror-struck tones. Then added: "My poor, misguided child!"

"Where is your sister, boy?" demanded Uncle Clarence thunderously.

"She's upstairs. I expect she is still asleep." David answered. He was still half asleep himself, and stifled a yawn behind his hand.

"David," shrieked Aunt Marion, "what have you done

to your clothes? Your good suit is quite ruined, and it cost a pretty penny!"

"What have you to say for yourself, you young rascal?" Uncle Clarence shouted indignantly. David, now fully awake, looked at Sholto, and saw that he was half smiling. He evidently found Uncle Clarence and Aunt Marion funny. Suddenly David saw that, far from being formidable, as he had always thought, they really were rather ridiculous.

"Answer me; don't stand there insolently staring!" Uncle Clarence roared.

"Well," David said in his quiet way, "we're sorry if we've caused you and Aunt Marion any anxiety——"

"Anxiety!" echoed Aunt Marion faintly, her hand on her heart.

David continued: "But we had to go, Kate and I, to bring the Prince to Tomay."

"The Prince?" queried Uncle Clarence. "What do you mean?"

"I mean the baby—the baby Prince. John Forester was rescuing him from the Protector, who had plotted to get rid of him. Kate and I thought you and Aunt Marion might not understand, so we set off for Tomay by ourselves at once."

"The idea!" exclaimed Aunt Marion. "When you had hardly been out of the city!"

"Well, it was quite all right, Aunt Marion," David said reassuringly. "Because Sholto helped us, and we found Uncle Hugh, and he helped us too."

"Ah, Clarence!" cried Aunt Marion dramatically. "I only hope we are not too late to save these poor children from the clutches of Hugh Winter."

"I don't see what is wrong with Uncle Hugh," argued David. "He has very kindly said that Kate and I can live with him."

"What ingratitude!" spluttered Uncle Clarence.

"Truly we aren't ungrateful," David said. "We both thank you very much for all that you have done for us, but you've found it a tedious bother really, haven't you? I mean, you were always saying what sacrifices you had to make and everything. And Uncle Hugh wants us to live with him. He's lonely all by himself, and Kate and I mean to help him run his cottage and small-holding at Dragon's End."

David made this long speech rather fast, because he could see that Uncle Clarence was all ready to interrupt. When he had finished his uncle and aunt stared at him as if he had suddenly gone mad. They couldn't have looked more surprised if he had suddenly sprouted horns and a tail.

"My dear boy——" Uncle Clarence was beginning, in tones of deep suffering, when Smith entered with a loaded tray, closely followed by Hugh with another. David turned to him eagerly.

"Uncle Hugh, Uncle Clarence and Aunt Marion are here. They've come to take Kate and me back to Ree City. But we can't go, can we?"

Sholto had left the room with Smith. Hugh put down his tray carefully and greeted his brother and sister-in-law, who replied coldly. Hugh then asked them if they had had a pleasant journey, but Uncle Clarence brushed the kindly enquiry aside and began to bluster.

"This ungrateful boy," he said, "does not seem to realize that his aunt and I have made a trying journey simply in order to take his sister and himself under our care. He does not seem to appreciate what we have done for them both all these years——"

"But I've told you, I do!" cried David in exasperation.

"David," Hugh said, "go and see how Kate is and ask her if she is coming down to breakfast or having it in bed."

David departed with an imploring look at Hugh. He found Kate looking much better. She had her arm in a sling and was sitting on a stool while Joanna did her hair.

"David, your head looks like a mop," commented the Princess. "You can have this comb in a minute."

"Something dreadful has happened!" cried David in great agitation. "Uncle Clarence and Aunt Marion have come to fetch us. They want to take us back to Ree City!"

"Oh no!" gasped Kate. "We can't! We've only just started to be alive. Oh, Your Highness"—she clutched Joanna's skirt as if she was drowning—"please help us."

"Dear Kate, don't look so desolated," Joanna said kindly. "I am quite sure everything will be all right. Hugh will never let you go. He will arrange something. But you must make yourself look a little tidier, David, or your uncle and aunt will think we are letting you grow into a savage, which would never do."

"I can't understand why they want us back," said David desperately. "They were always going on about what a trial it was to bring us up. . . ."

"Well, perhaps we can persuade them to let you stay here," Joanna said, and her use of the pronoun "we" comforted them a little. They followed her downstairs, and in the hall they found the Prince of Tomay talking to Sholto. Kate, who was not in the least in awe of him, ran to him and poured out the doleful tidings.

"Oh, sir, please make them let us stay," she pleaded, for she believed implicitly that he could do anything he set out to do.

"Don't worry, Kate," he reassured her, "Hugh will talk them round. Come and have some breakfast. You should be hungry after last night's alarums and excursions."

Kate entered the farm parlour bristling with hostility. She felt hot and prickly with misery and resentment at Aunt Marion's appearing in her life again and threatening her with all the old restrictions.

"Ah, here is Kate," she heard Uncle Hugh say. "Come along, Kate, and see your Aunt Marion."

Kate went forward, and Aunt Marion pecked her cheek, and said in a chilly voice, "Well, Kate, I hear that you and David wish to stay in Tomay."

"Oh yes, Aunt Marion," blurted Kate, and added as an afterthought, "please. . . ."

"Well, Kate," Aunt Marion said, "your Uncle Clarence and I think you and David are very ungrateful to us when we have done so much for you. However, if Hugh wishes to care for a thankless child I suppose David may stay here, though he will not have the advantages he has had in Ree City," she sniffed, and looked scornfully at David, and then proceeded. "But your Uncle Clarence and I, Kate, do not feel that it is the life for a girl. You and Fanny are company for each other, and you must be brought up as befits your station."

"I haven't got a station!" cried Kate indignantly. "You

can't separate us." Her voice shook, and her sight blurred with the tears she kept back. She heard Joanna speaking.

"Mistress Holt, if you won't trust Kate to Hugh, would you let me have her, perhaps? I promise that I would take great care of her and see that she learns all the things a young lady should, and then she would be near enough to David to see him often."

Aunt Marion seemed very much taken aback by such an offer from a great lady for Kate, of all people. Now, if it had been Fanny!

"Well, Your Highness is most kind," she said, "but what poor Fanny, my own little daughter, would say if she thought she was losing her dear little playmate for ever, I cannot bear to think!"

"Then perhaps if you could spare me Kate, she and Fanny could exchange visits," suggested Joanna guilefully.

The prospect of Fanny's moving in such high society was too much for Aunt Marion, and she gave way. Kate, radiant, embraced first Joanna, as well as she could with one arm, and then her Aunt. It was the first spontaneous caress she had given Aunt Marion since years ago her baby affection had been snubbed, and it was not well received. Aunt Marion shrieked faintly:

"Child! What a hoyden you are!" she exclaimed in shocked tones, but Kate was too happy to care.

"And now, what about breakfast?" suggested Sholto hungrily.

At that moment Smith entered.

"His Majesty will join you for breakfast," he announced pompously, and added "and 'is nibs is yelling."

Joanna went to fetch the baby and then they all "breakfasted" together.

Uncle Clarence and Aunt Marion were in the minority as the skeletons at the feast, as David said afterwards, but nobody troubled about their disapproving stiffness. Even King Roderick was cheerful and friendly in a quiet way, and the baby shouted with laughter and banged on the table with a spoon. As for David and Kate, they were so blissfully happy that not all the uncles and aunts in the world could have spoiled their delight.

"Since we started this adventure I haven't once had breakfast at the proper time!" David remarked triumphantly.

"Aha," said Hugh, "but we'll start being punctual tomorrow. Don't forget I'm a schoolmaster. You don't know what you're in for!"

"Oh dear!" exclaimed David in such rueful tones that every one except the uncle and aunt laughed.

"There is just one thing before David and Kate are returned to the schoolroom," the King said. "If we've all finished breakfast, I suggest we adjourn to the garden."

He had suddenly, from being an ordinary, rather quiet person, become a King. As he rose they all did too, and the women curtseyed and the men bowed as he passed to the door. There he paused and held out his hand to Kate.

"Come, Kate," he said, looking down at her, his face grave, his eyes a little wistful. From feeling momentarily shy at being so singled out, Kate, seeing the expression in his eyes, suddenly felt sorry for him. She smiled up at him, and feeling greatly honoured, left the room with her good hand in his. The others followed.

"In my son's name and my own," His Majesty began, as he turned to face them all on the grass in the autumn sunshine, "I should like to thank my most loyal subjects. I don't think," he added sadly, "that I have been as faithful to my people as they have been to me. Of my cousin of Tomay I must ask forgiveness. I once banished you." He paused.

"That was well enough deserved, sire," Tomay said quickly. "If I had not left the court in—" he smiled ruefully—"in a temper, the misunderstanding might never have arisen—and in any case I shall always be grateful for that sentence, since it found me Joanna."

"I too, sire," Joanna put in.

"Nevertheless it was a fault," the King insisted.

"Not all on one side," answered Adrian firmly.

The King's face crumpled into a smile.

"You still refuse to give in, Cousin Adrian," he remarked.

Tomay, caught out, laughed, and admitted defeat with a gesture. Joanna slid her hand into his, and Sholto murmured wickedly:

"These unmanageable nobles!"

"Ah, Sholto St. George." King Roderick had heard that remark. "Come forward if you please. You will have less cause to sneer at the nobility in future," he went on, his eyes full of laughter. "For I intend to create you Duke of Craglands in place of Rupert Montmaris, now attainted."

Sholto looked completely flabbergasted.

"Sire," he exclaimed at last, "you must be joking—me—a foundling, and most probably a gipsy at that!"

"A gipsy I have found loyal," the King said, holding

out his hand. Sholto bent his knee and kissed it, completely silenced for once.

"And now, last but not least, David and Kate," the King went on, becoming far less formal. "I think Master Winter would judge you too young for ennoblement, but I will not forget you, and neither, I dare promise, shall my son, for whom you braved so much. Come back to Ree City later, if you can bear to leave the forest, and we will prove it. In the meantime I must ask you to accept these gifts as a memento of your Prince."

So saying he handed to David a gold ring he had worn on his own finger, and clasped a bracelet on to Kate's thin wrist. She gazed at it for a moment speechless with delight, while David was thanking His Majesty, and turned her wrist so that the bright sapphires glowed and sparkled.

"It was the Queen's," Roderick explained gently. "She would have wanted you to have it."

"And I gave my other one away!" cried Kate. "Oh, thank you, thank you!"

Quite overcome, she felt on the edge of bursting into sobs, and fled to Tomay, her usual refuge. Inside the comforting circle of his arm she was able to stifle her tears against his coat, blink them away and secretly admire the bracelet while the others were all talking at once, and congratulating and teasing Sholto by calling him "Your Grace," a form of address to which he did not take very kindly.